NIPS Go National

Takeaways

Are You Listening?, Lydia Sturton
Artists Are Crazy and Other Stories, Ken Catran
Blue Fin, Colin Thiele
The Changeling, Gail Merritt
Chickenpox, Yuck!, Josie Montano
The Dog King, Paul Collins
Dragon's Tear, Sue Lawson
Fake ID, Hazel Edwards
Fries, Ken Catran
Get a Life!, Krista Bell
The Grandfather Clock, Anthony Hill
The Great Ferret Race, Paul Collins
It's Time, Cassandra Klein, Karen R. Brooks
Jodie's Journey, Colin Thiele
The Keeper, Rosanne Hawke
Landslide, Colin Thiele
The Lyrebird's Tail, Susan Robinson
Mystery at Devon House, Cory Daniells
Monstered, Bernie Monagle
Ned's Kang-u-roo, Vashti Farrer
NewBjorn, Kathryn England
NIPS XI, Ruth Starke
NIPS Go National, Ruth Starke
No Regrets, Krista Bell
Pop Starlets, Josie Montano
Read My Mind!, Krista Bell
The Rescue of Princess Athena, Kathryn England
Sailmaker, Rosanne Hawke
Saving Saddler Street, Ruth Starke
The Sea Caves, Colin Thiele
Seashores and Shadows, Colin Thiele
Space Games, Mike Carter
Spy Babies, Ian Bone
Swan Song, Colin Thiele
Timmy, Colin Thiele
Twice upon a Time, John Pinkney
Wendy's Whale, Colin Thiele
Who Cares?, Krista Bell
The Worst Year of My Life, Katherine Goode

NIPS Go National

Ruth Starke

For Petra

Acknowledgements

I'm no cricket expert, and am therefore immensely grateful to everybody whose knowledge, insights and advice helped me to write this book. I'd like to thank Megan Smith, Project Officer, Game Development, and Meredith Kelly, Administration Assistant, Development and Coaching, Australian Cricket Board; Harvey Jolly, Cricket Operations Manager, and Bernard Whimpress, Museum Curator, South Australian Cricket Association; Alex Warneke and Barbara Intini, Prince Alfred College, Adelaide; the librarians at Unley and Goodwood Libraries; Barry Nicholls; and, above all, Bill 'Swampy' Marsh. Any mistakes and errors are my own, but there would be many more of them without his informed, generous and invaluable input. My thanks also to Pam Macintyre and Petra Starke, who read the manuscript and offered excellent advice, and to my editor, Helen Chamberlin.

Readers of Steve Waugh's *No Regrets: A Captain's Diary* (Harper Sports, 1999) and *Ashes Diary* (Ironbark, 1993) will recognise the inspiration for Lan's diary entries and the Nips' poems.

Thomas C. Lothian Pty Ltd
132 Albert Road, South Melbourne, Victoria 3205
www.lothian.com.au
www.ruthstarke.itgo.com

First published 2003
Reprinted 2003 (twice)

National Library of Australia
Cataloguing-in-publication data:

Starke, Ruth, 1946-.
Nips go national.

For upper primary/lower secondary school age children.
ISBN 0 7344 0474 3 (pbk).

1. Cricket players -Juvenile fiction. 2. Cricket matches - Juvenile fiction.
3. Ethnic relations - Juvenile fiction. I. Title. (Series: Takeaways).

A823.3

Cover design by Michelle Mackintosh
Photography by Sonya Pletes
Illustrations by Annie Mertzlin
Book design by Paulene Meyer
Printed in Australia by Griffin Press

One

Day Four, Australia v England, Melbourne Cricket Ground

All out for 123. It's an extraordinary collapse by the Australians.

In the tea-break, the captain approaches spin bowler Lan Nguyen.

'Australia's in trouble,' he says grimly. 'It's a dog of a wicket and their bowlers exploited it superbly. We threw away a winning position. England's got eight hours to make 137 to win. Which they will, unless ...' He looks at Nguyen and the appeal is in his eyes as well as his voice. 'What we need now is a miracle. I'm looking to you, mate. It's a big ask, I know.'

Nguyen's gaze doesn't falter. 'I'll do my best, Captain.'

'But your shoulder ... You copped some savage bouncers. Almost bodyline. They were out to get you.'

Nguyen shrugs, ignoring the pain. It will mean surgery after the match but that's a small price to pay for his country and, in the meantime ... 'I'm fine,' he says. 'What's your game plan?'

'Just go out there and take wickets.'

Nguyen nods. 'I'm a bowler. That's what I do.'

'Good man.'

He leads the team back onto the field. The home crowd is unimpressed with 123 and there are few cheers.

The England captain strolls to the wicket.

Nguyen breathes deeply and secretly flexes his spinning finger. It's sore, possibly fractured, but this is no time for first aid. Take out the captain and Australia has a chance, he thinks. Why not bowl up a flipper first ball? It's a risky decision. If he doesn't get it spot on it could be hit for a four or a six; the fielders will lose confidence. It will be the beginning of the end.

He bowls.

The batsman sees the ball bounce on a length that looks perfect for a sweep to the boundary. He smiles and lifts his bat. But the ball is coming at him faster than he expects, and then it seems to drift in the air, like a balloon slowly losing air. He's forced to hold his bat stiffly, waiting for the ball to spin from right to left.

It doesn't. It flies straight on, sneaking between his pad and bat and smashing the stumps. It's the perfect flipper. Perhaps the best flipper ever bowled.

Nguyen punches the air with delight.

The batsman looks stunned. What just happened?

The MCG crowd have come alive. They're on their feet, chanting, cheering, waving the flag. His team mates are rushing to him. Everyone's giving him high fives.

'Well bowled, mate,' the captain says quietly, and shakes his hand. 'I knew I could rely on you.'

'One down, nine to go,' says Nguyen.

Out comes the new batsman, fear in his eyes …

'Nguyen, I don't know where you are right now, but it's certainly not in the classroom. Perhaps you'd care to enlighten us?'

Lan came out of his daydream and found Mr Thistleton glaring at him. For a split-second, he considered actually telling him. Mr Thistleton was a cricket fan, after all. 'I was at the MCG, sir, winning the Test for Australia.' Just as quickly he decided that honesty was unlikely to be the best policy. Mr Thistleton's expression was not that of a man eager to hear the sporting fabrications of a student whose best grade in Ancient History was a C minus.

'Sorry, sir,' he said meekly.

'You've heard of Aristotle, I take it, Nguyen?'

Reluctantly, Lan left the second batsman at the crease and turned his mind to the question. 'I've *heard* of him, sir,' he said cautiously. 'Um, wasn't he an ancient Greek?'

The class tittered.

'We've moved on from that fundamental point, Nguyen, and if you'd been paying attention you would have moved on with us,' said Mr Thistleton. 'Aristotle was a Greek scholar who lived about 400 BC. We were discussing his views on women. What were those views, Nguyen?'

Views on women? What did that mean? He hazarded a guess. 'Um, he was in favour of them?'

The class roared. Mr Thistleton rapped on his desk. 'Aristotle held that females were inferior to males, but if he was in this classroom now, Nguyen, I think he might revise that view. In ancient Greece, however, women were indeed considered inferior to men in all areas of life.'

Lisa Huynh's hand shot up. 'Not in having babies, sir! Women were pretty superior in that.'

'Big deal,' jeered Ryan West, but Mr Thistleton conceded the point. 'But socially, politically and intellectually, women were considered inferior. Greece was a warrior culture, and women's lack of physical strength prevented their participation in war. Nor were they considered intelligent enough to govern.'

'Right on!' crowed Ryan West, raising his fist in the air.

Lisa scowled at him. 'What did women do, sir? Besides have babies?'

'Their work was largely domestic. They cooked, kept the house in order, looked after children, fetched water. Decorated pots and vases of the period show women spinning and weaving.'

Things hadn't changed much, Lan reflected. His mother still did all those things, although she had a sewing machine. He was glad he was a boy. The only spinning he was interested in was on the cricket pitch.

'Of course, there were exceptions,' Mr Thistleton went on, seeing Lisa's expression. 'A woman called Agnodice disguised herself as a man in order to practise medicine. She was so good that patients flocked to her, and other doctors became jealous and suspicious. They took her to court where the truth was revealed, and she was prosecuted. But her patients protested and she was later acquitted.'

'So women have to be better than men to succeed?' Lisa said. 'They can't just be as good, or average?'

'Well ...' said Mr Thistleton.

Lan's thoughts were still running on cricket. He raised his hand. 'Did women in ancient Greece play sport, sir?'

Mr Thistleton felt on safer ground here. 'Definitely not. It would have been unthinkable. And even if a woman did want to run or throw a discus, athletes usually performed naked, so disguise was out of the question.'

Ryan West and Adam Morris sniggered. Ryan picked up his pencil and flipped open his exercise pad.

'I don't think an illustration will be necessary, thank you, West,' Mr Thistleton said, fixing him with a steely glance. Ryan dropped his pencil.

'That's enough about what women didn't do,' the teacher said firmly. 'Let's move on to what they did do. I have some overheads here of glazed pots which illustrate aspects of women's life. The first shows an Athenian wedding procession about 440 BC ...'

The overhead was upside down and Lan's mind switched off again. He wasn't interested in weddings, and especially not when a capacity crowd at the MCG was holding its collective breath for the start of his next over. What sort of ball should he bowl? The batsman would be expecting another flipper, so maybe a standard leg break? Maybe two or three leg breaks, and *then* another flipper?

The wedding procession disappeared, to be replaced by a fuzzy picture of women mourning at a funeral. Mr Thistleton fiddled with the knob while the class fidgeted and weeping Athenian matrons came in and out of focus. There was a knock on the door and a junior student came in, clutching a note.

'Message from Mr Drummond, sir.'

'Thank you. Leave it on my desk,' said Mr Thistleton.

'He said it was urgent, sir.'

'Oh very well, bring it here.'

The student delivered the note and scuttled out of the classroom. Mr Thistleton unfolded the paper and read it, frowning. 'I must say I don't see what the particular urgency is, but the principal wants to see you in his office, Nguyen.'

At yet another mention of his name, Lan's mind was once more jerked back from the MCG. What was Old Thistleton asking him now? What had he been talking about? He frowned with deep concentration at the screen as if fascinated by ancient Greek burial customs.

'Well, get along,' said Mr Thistleton briskly. 'If the principal says it's urgent, he wants to see you now, not this time next week.'

'Yes, sir.' Lan got to his feet, grateful his knowledge of ancient history wasn't to be publicly tested again but nervous about what the summons might mean. His mind raced over more recent history. Had he done anything to attract the attention of Mr Drummond?

His best friend, Izram Hussein, screwed his face into what was obviously meant to be an expression of sympathy and solidarity, but looked instead as if he'd just bitten into a hot chilli. Ryan West grinned maliciously and muttered, 'You're in for it,' as Lan passed his desk.

Lisa Huynh, who'd been looking to pay Ryan back, said loudly and indignantly, 'Why should Lan have done something bad? If it's urgent, someone in his family could be ill or had an accident, couldn't they, sir?'

Lan stopped in his tracks. Mr Thistleton had now managed to adjust the projector's focus knob and the overhead of the Athenian funeral suddenly sprang into sharp relief on the screen. Lan stared aghast at the tomb and the wagon carrying the body.

Mr Thistleton was about to tell Lisa not to be so silly, of course nothing like that had happened, but he paused. How did he know? It was possible, wasn't it?

He whipped off the overhead of the funeral and replaced it with one of women with urns around a fountain. 'Get along, Lan,' he said kindly. 'I'm sure it's nothing of the sort.'

Lan didn't miss the change of tone and it convinced him that some terrible accident had indeed happened. Perhaps crates of coconuts had fallen on his father's head as he was unloading at the shop and he was now in a coma in hospital. Perhaps his mother had been electrocuted at her sewing machine; she always overloaded the power board in the garage. Perhaps one of the twins had chased a ball into Dunrobin Street and been mowed down by a speeding car. By the time he'd raced, panting, into the administration block he'd run through a dozen fatal scenarios.

In the front office Mrs Moody looked up from her computer and greeted him with a smile. 'Hello, Lan, you're in a hurry. How's the bowling going?'

Lan's mood lightened. Mrs Moody would hardly smile and enquire about his bowling if the principal was about to inform him that unfortunately he was now an orphan. And Mr Drummond would have warned her: 'Have a glass of water standing by in case he collapses,' he would have said. 'I have to tell Nguyen that his parents have been killed by a crazed gunman and his brother and sister kidnapped.' Lan looked at her desk. He couldn't see a glass of water and Mrs Moody was still smiling at him.

'Getting better,' he said, trying to slow his breathing. 'Um, Mr Drummond wants to see me. D'you know what it's about?'

Mrs Moody looked mysterious. 'I'll let him tell you.'

She got up and Lan followed her down the corridor. She knocked lightly on the principal's door and stuck her head into his office. 'Lan Nguyen's here to see you, Mr Drummond.' She nodded to Lan that he should go in and then closed the door behind him.

The principal, seated behind his desk and seemingly occupied with scrawling his signature on various documents, barely looked up but indicated with a wave of his hand that Lan should seat himself. Lan sat and waited, certain now that nothing terrible had happened to any member of his family. Surely not even Mr Drummond would go on signing papers and let him sit there in ignorance if it had.

The principal eventually capped his pen, shuffled the papers together, and looked up. 'Ah, Lan,' he said, as if surprised to see him sitting there. 'How's the cricket going?'

'All right, sir.'

'Keeping up the … er, practice, are you? You and the team?'

'The Nips, sir? Yes, sir.'

A flicker of distaste registered on the principal's face. He still didn't like the name but he could hardly complain when it was formed from the initials of North Illaba Primary School. Nothing to do, apparently, with the fact that the team was almost exclusively made up of students from Asian backgrounds. Well, they wouldn't be his concern much longer. The last days of the final term were approaching and next year most of them would be going to North Illaba High School (the NIHS?) and he'd be able to forget about cricket and the embarrassment of that unfortunate name. In the meantime …

He removed a document from the pile in front of him and scanned it again, even though he'd read it through twice already. 'I've received this letter,' he said.

Lan's anxiety rose a few degrees. Obviously his family had suffered no terrible accident — the news was unlikely to be conveyed by letter — although he supposed it could be a ransom note. But why send it to Mr Drummond? More likely to be a complaint of some sort, perhaps from one of the property owners whose yard backed onto the eastern boundary of the oval. Balls were always being whacked or kicked over the fences. There was a school rule against trespass but everybody ignored it: balls were too valuable to abandon. A little frown was drawing Mr Drummond's caterpillar eyebrows together so probably somebody's plants had been flattened.

In fact, the principal was frowning because he was perplexed. When he'd first sighted the letter, he'd quickly taken in the thick cream paper and the green and gold embossed letterhead of a kangaroo and emu holding a shield and assumed in some excitement that the prime minister was writing to him. A closer look had proved this not to be the case, but he had still been impressed, despite himself. Few letters of such magnificence landed on his desk.

'… this letter from the Australian Cricket Board,' he continued. 'From the General Manager, Game Development.'

Lan's mouth fell open.

'He's interested in your team, for some reason.'

Lan nearly fell off his chair.

'I'm surprised he heard about our little game,' Mr Drummond said, stroking his chin and narrowing his eyes at Lan. 'Did you send a report to the Australian Cricket Board?'

'Gosh, no,' said Lan. As if! The idea had never occurred to him. Why would the ACB be interested in a school cricket match? Although in his eyes and the eyes of the other Nips, it certainly hadn't been a 'little' game. 'It was probably all the publicity we got, sir. You know, the TV crews that came to the school and the stories about Spinner — Mr McGinty — in the papers.'

'Ah, yes.' In the week or so since the match the principal had all but forgotten about the old chap everybody had made such a fuss about. What was he, some former Test player? The boys had discovered him sleeping in a corner of the local library and somehow persuaded him to be their coach. The level of media interest had been amazing. Typical, of course. Nobody wanted to know about deteriorating buildings, large class sizes and widening gaps in primary school education, but resurrect some old forgotten sporting has-been and the media beat a path to your door.

He scanned the letter again. And obviously there was money to burn, as long as you used the magic words 'cultural diversity'. He looked up at Lan, who could hardly contain his curiosity. 'Apparently there's a federal program called "Living in Harmony". The Department of Immigration and Multicultural Affairs have got together with the Australian Cricket Board to —' he consulted the letter again — '*use sport in multicultural communities to promote greater understanding and harmony between cultures*. Ms Trad will know all about that.

The point is, they're running some interstate cricket carnival and have invited selected teams from around the country, including yours, to compete for something called the Harmony Cup. Interested?'

Was the Pope Catholic? Of course he was interested! Lan nodded vigorously. 'It's a great honour, sir.'

'Hmmm. I suppose it is.' Privately the principal considered the whole thing rather discriminatory if, as the letter implied, only indigenous and culturally diverse teams were involved. What did that say about the so-called level playing field?

'Would we have to go to Canberra, sir?' Lan asked.

'Canberra? No, no. Melbourne.'

Lan's eyes widened. Hadn't he, just fifteen minutes ago, been dreaming of cricketing glory at the MCG? It was a sign, it had to be. 'Wow!' he breathed. 'Imagine the Nips at the MCG. Spinner will be rapt!'

'I think it's highly unlikely that schoolboy teams will get anywhere near the MCG,' Mr Drummond said. 'You might have to set your sights a little lower.'

'Does it say in the letter, sir?'

'No, the letter merely asks for a registration of interest and says details will then be forwarded. The event will be held over three days in mid-January, during the summer holidays.'

That was only about a month away. Oh definitely, the Nips had to go. He could hardly wait to tell them, and to tell his parents. They'd be so proud. Except … He knew the first question his mother would ask.

'It'll cost a lot of money, won't it, sir?' Lan asked anxiously. 'Melbourne's a long way and we'd have to stay at a hotel, and pay for food and stuff.'

'That seems to have been taken care of.' Mr Drummond consulted the letter. 'Interstate teams will be accommodated in the boarding house of St Paul's Grammar School; meals, transport, and all equipment will be provided, although players are free to bring their own. It seems that your only expense will be getting to Melbourne, and there's even subsidies available for that if needed.'

'Wow! The government's being really generous.'

'Indeed. Amazing how there's always money for this sort of thing. Anyway, the point is, by next January you and the other boys will no longer be members of this school. Your days at North Illaba Primary will officially end next week. Which means that the school cannot be responsible for you should you decide to accept this invitation. Do you understand?'

Lan frowned. 'Not really, sir.'

'This can't be regarded as an official school excursion, nor can I assign a teacher to accompany the team. You'll need at least one responsible adult to go with you, perhaps two. That will be for you to arrange. Possibly a parent?'

'Oh, Spinner — Mr McGinty, that is — will come with us for sure, sir. He's our coach. He won't want to miss out on this.'

'Well, that's for you to decide,' the principal said. Old McGinty certainly wasn't his idea of a suitable supervisor for a group of boisterous boys, some of whom could barely speak English — God knows what problems lay ahead or what mischief they'd get up to — but it was hardly his concern.

He passed the letter across the desk to Lan. 'You might as well have this. I suggest you talk it over with the other boys and with your parents and then inform Mrs Moody of your decision. She can then reply on your behalf. From then on, it's between you and them.' And the school can get back to normal and forget all this fuss about one of the most boring sports ever invented, he added silently.

'Thanks, sir.' Lan took the letter as if it were a sacred object, which irritated Mr Drummond even more.

'You may return to class.'

'Yes, sir.'

As he was passing the front office Mrs Moody,

looking as pleased as if she'd been invited to Melbourne too, said, 'Congratulations, Lan! Aren't you thrilled?'

'You bet! I thought it was going to be bad news. Why did Mr Drummond say it was urgent?'

'Urgent?'

'He sent a message saying he had to see me urgently.'

'And you thought the worst?' Mrs Moody gave a sympathetic shake of her head. 'He has a Rotary lunch, that's all. I guess he wants to get away quickly.'

Lan was too happy to feel annoyed.

Two

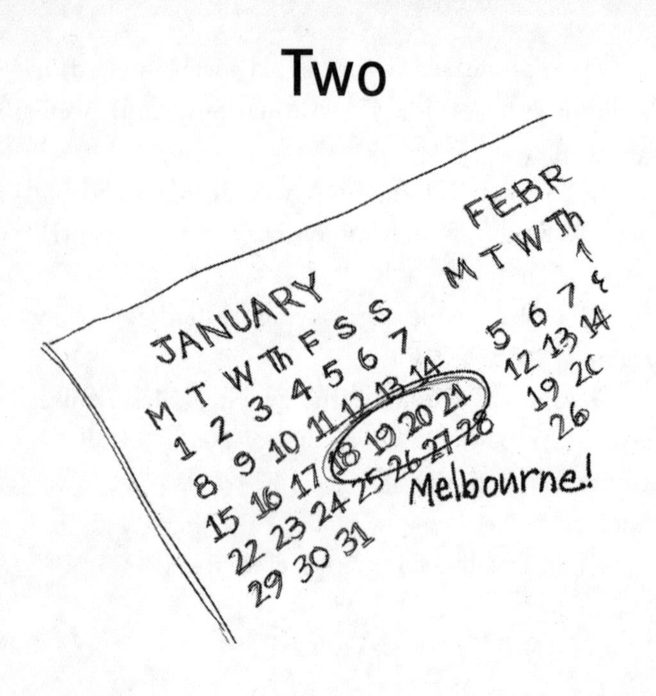

It was impossible to keep such thrilling news to himself. Lan briefly considered waiting until he could get all the Nips together in order to tell them first, then decided that he couldn't possibly wait that long. Besides, several of them were back in Mr Thistleton's class, no doubt bored witless by all the upside-down and unfocused overheads of ancient Greek women. He owed it to them to provide an exciting diversion.

He entered the room bearing the letter in front of him, with its impressive green and gold shield for all to see. Had it been a message from the gods he could not have looked more awed or reverential. And just in case they missed the significance of the letterhead, he pretended to fumble it just as he passed Ryan West's desk.

'Oops!' he said loudly. 'Nearly dropped this official invitation from the **Australian Cricket Board**.'

There was a stir of interest from everyone in the class except Ryan, who was determined not to be impressed. 'An invitation to what? A beginners' coaching clinic?' he sneered. Which was more or less exactly what Lan had hoped he'd say. Now he had an excuse for telling his news without sounding like a bighead.

He told them.

The biggest grins came from his team mates, Izram, Andy Chen, Hiroki Yoshida and Akram Rajavi, but their collective excitement was nearly eclipsed by Mr Thistleton's enthusiastic reaction. 'My goodness, boys, what an honour! The Australian Cricket Board! Well, I never! Congratulations are certainly in order! Class, all together, "Congratulations, Nips XI."' He stared very hard at Ryan West.

'Congratulations Nips XI!' they chanted. Even Ryan.

Lan grinned. This was shaping up to be one of the best days of his life.

'May I see the letter?' Mr Thistleton read it, exclaiming to himself as he did. 'Harmony Cup, how interesting ... indigenous teams too, I see ... St Paul's Grammar, very prestigious ...'

Behind him, and at the back of the class, Andy Chen took the opportunity to reach down and disconnect the power to the overhead projector. They'd had quite enough of *that* for one day.

'Well, Lan, this will certainly help to put cricket back on the school agenda,' Mr Thistleton said, returning the letter to him. 'I trust the principal was suitably impressed?'

Lan considered. It was hard to figure out precisely what Mr Drummond's reaction had been but he didn't think *impressed* was the right word. 'He said he supposed it was an honour but it didn't have anything to do with the school.'

Mr Thistleton looked surprised. 'Whatever did he mean?'

'The carnival's next January and we'll have left here by then, sir.'

'So?'

'So he said we could go if we wanted but it had nothing to do with the school.'

'Extraordinary. The principal has a very individual way of looking at things sometimes.' Mr Thistleton shook his head and slid another transparency onto the overhead projector. Really, it was easier to understand the mindset of an ancient Athenian than of someone like Mr Drummond. 'All right, class, back to work. Here we have a vase, circa 550BC … No, we don't. Complete darkness. Dear, dear, what's wrong with this thing now?'

Andy spoke up. 'Sir, it's nearly lunch time, sir. Can we go please?'

Mr Thistleton jiggled the on-off switch and sighed in frustration. 'Oh, very well. I'll have to take this machine to the workshop and see if someone can fix it.'

The news flew around the school faster than a Brett Lee delivery. So many people wanted to see the famous letter that Lan slipped it into a plastic sleeve to protect it. Ms Trad was especially thrilled. 'It doesn't matter whether you win the Cup or not,' she said. 'What matters is that by taking part you and the other teams are helping to build an inclusive and harmonious nation.'

Well yeah, thought Lan, but we want to win, too.

Tomas Nuñez could hardly contain his excitement, even though Lan wasn't certain he'd grasped all the details. His English had improved a lot since he'd arrived at North Illaba from El Salvador last term, but it was difficult to convey the concept of community harmony and the prestige of the Australian Cricket Board in words that he would understand. Lan decided to leave that to Ms Trad.

'Hey, Onya. The Nips are going to Melbourne to play cricket, what d'you think of that?'

Tomas beamed and gave him the thumbs up. 'Cricket. Melbourne. Yes please. I think we win. Onya, Lan!'

Lan grinned and returned the gesture. 'Onya' had been one of the first Australian expressions Tomas had learnt and it had become his nickname in the team. Of course, ever since Spinner had been their coach, all of them had picked up a lot of Australian expressions. His own vocabulary had been very usefully increased.

'We have to tell Spinner,' Lan said to Izram. 'What about after school? He ought to be home then.'

Izram agreed. 'And don't forget David.'

David Ho, their best player, attended another school. They had met him at the season try-outs at the Illaba Cricket Club where, much to their surprise, he'd decided to join their newly-formed Nips XI rather than either of the club teams. It had been a lucky break for the rookie team and Lan in particular. Not only was David a strong batsman with his own bat (the only one they had in those early days) but Mr Ho's generosity had helped to provide their team uniforms, and his enthusiasm for sport had helped persuade Lan's parents that there was more to life than work and study.

'I'll ring David tonight,' Lan promised. 'And we have to tell Grace, too.'

There were so many people they had to tell but Grace, the librarian at the Illaba Library, came very near the top of the list. If it hadn't been for Grace, Lan would never have known about the cricket club tryouts and then he'd never have met David and even more importantly, he and Izram would never have met the famous Clarence McGinty. Lan could still hear her voice as she tapped the scruffy old man, seemingly asleep in the corner of the library, on the shoulder. *Spinner, there's a couple of young cricketers I'd like you to meet.* How shocked he and Izzie had been.

Which only went to prove how deceptive appearances could be. Spinner's glory days might be behind him but he knew how to inspire and he knew how to coach. The Nips could never have come all this way without him.

'We might have time to go to the library after we see Spinner,' Lan said.

But when they got to Spinner's house, which wasn't far from the Denby Reserve where they had cricket practice, Grace was there. The two of them were having a cup of tea in the kitchen: Lan could see them from the side window. He tapped on it and the little black and white fox terrier under the table pricked up his ears. Spinner rose and went to the back door to let them in.

'Yer ears must be burnin',' he said.

'No,' Lan said, puzzled. 'That's why we have to wear a school hat.' Couldn't Spinner *see* he was? No, maybe not. He wasn't wearing his glasses. There they were on the top of his head.

'We were just talkin' about you,' Spinner said. 'Come in.'

'Talking about me? Why? Did you get a letter too?' Lan asked.

'A letter?'

The boys followed him into the kitchen and exchanged greetings with Grace. Larri wagged his tail, eager for attention. Lan spotted a letter and envelope among the tea things on the table. 'You did get a letter!' he exclaimed. He was disappointed. So much for breaking the big news.

Spinner looked taken aback. He glanced across at Grace, who gave a puzzled little shake of her head.

'An old friend saw something in the paper about the King's match and wrote to me, that's all.'

Spinner picked up the letter, folded it into its envelope and slipped it into his pocket.

Lan, relieved, said, 'Now I can see it's not a bit like the one I got.'

'You got a letter too?' Grace asked.

'Yeah.' Why were the two of them so surprised? Millions of people got millions of letters every day, it was hardly a big coincidence. He pulled it out of his school bag and removed it from the plastic sleeve. OK, not many of them got letters as impressive as this one.

'From the Australian Cricket Board,' he announced proudly.

'We're invited to Melbourne,' Izram said.

'To play cricket,' Lan added.

'Next January.'

'For a Cup.'

'All expenses paid. Well, most of them.'

'Well, strike me pink!' Spinner's head was swivelling back and forth between them like a spectator watching a rapid tennis volley. 'Give us a look at this invite. Where are me specs?'

'On your head,' Grace said, smiling at the boys. 'Well done! You're going to go, of course?'

'You bet,' Lan said. 'And Spinner too.'

'I dunno about that.' He ran his eyes over the letter and then passed it to Grace. 'Seems to me the invitation's for the team, and probably a teacher. It's addressed to the school.'

'Only 'cos they didn't know any other address,' Izram said.

'And this is our last week at North Illaba,' Lan added. He told them of his conversation with Mr Drummond. 'So you gotta come, Spinner. Even if a teacher came with us, we'd still want you along. I don't reckon we could win a match without you there.'

'Ah, get away.'

Izram nodded his head in agreement. 'Teams that go on tour always take the coach along.'

'Not old crocks like me.'

'Yes they do,' Izram confirmed.

Spinner looked across the table at Grace. 'Melbourne,' he said.

Grace reached across and squeezed his hand. 'Go for it.'

'Who'd look after Larri?'

'I would, of course. It's only for four days.'

'I dunno. It's been a long time.'

'All the more reason to go.'

Spinner looked at the boys. 'I'll give it some serious consideration.'

'Does that mean you'll come?' Lan asked.

'It means I'll think it over, orright?'

What was there to think over, Lan wondered.

It wasn't as if Spinner had a family to consider or a barnyard of animals to take care of or a job to go to every day. It must be his age, he decided. When people got as old as Spinner, travelling sometimes became a problem. That's why there were special seats for the aged on public transport and wheelchairs at airports.

'We could get you a wheelchair,' he offered.

'A wheelchair! Gawd, why don't you get me an ambulance, too, while you're about it?' Spinner spluttered. 'And drive me straight to the cemetery to save time.'

Grace laughed. 'Go and cut the boys some of your Christmas cake,' she said. When he'd departed, grumbling, she leant across the table and lowered her voice. 'You get the rest of the team organised and leave Spinner to me. I'll persuade him.'

'Why doesn't he want to go?' Lan whispered back.

'He does, really. It's just something … personal. Leave it to me.'

'You boys want something to drink?' Spinner stood at the open door of the fridge.

Lan looked up. 'No, thanks. Cake'll be fine.'

Spinner cut them thick slabs of rich dark fruit cake. 'Get stuck into this. WG bakes me a cake every Christmas and it's always a ripper. She oughta be a cook, not a librarian.'

Grace blushed. The boys each took a slice. 'It's very good,' Lan said, even though the cake was slightly sticky and stuck to the top of his mouth.

'The icing's nice,' Izram said.

'Is it a special Christmas food? You know, like roast turkey?' Lan asked. Not that he'd ever eaten turkey. Being Vietnamese, the Nguyen family paid only scant regard to the traditions of Christmas, and his mother was as likely to put a roast turkey on the dinner table as a baked and stuffed football.

'It's traditional to have a fruit cake,' Grace said. 'It's an old custom from the northern hemisphere where December is very cold and there's no fresh fruit. So dried fruit is baked in a cake.'

'And the white icing on the cake is like snow on the ground,' said Izram, inspecting his slice.

'Probably. I never thought of that.'

'We oughta go,' Lan said. 'We haven't told our parents yet. Or David.'

'Take some cake home with you,' Spinner offered.

Lan could see that Izram was about to accept, so he kicked him under the table and said quickly, 'Oh, that's OK, Spinner, we've got plenty of cake at home. Thanks anyway.'

They said their goodbyes and Grace repeated her congratulations.

'Christmas or no Christmas, you'll have to get

off your backsides and put in some serious practice,' Spinner warned.

'You bet!' Lan could think of no better way to spend his summer.

When they were out on the street, Izram turned on him. 'Why'd you kick me like that?'

''Cos you were going to take his cake.'

'So? He offered it. *Oh no, Spinner, we've got plenty of cake at home*. What was all that about? I haven't got any cake at home.'

'First of all, he's an old man who's hardly got any food. Didn't you see how empty his fridge was? Second, Grace made that cake for him, not us. It might be the only thing he'll have to eat all Christmas.'

Izram looked suitably chastened. 'I didn't think of that. He can come round to the Bukhara. We're closed on Christmas Day but he can still eat with us. I'll ask him.'

'Do you eat turkey?'

'Nah. Curries and stuff. Just more of them.'

Lan nodded. Spinner loved Mr Hussein's vindaloo. They walked on to the corner of Denby Street and stopped to watch the club teams at net practice.

'Spinner doesn't seem very keen to come with us to Melbourne, does he?' Lan said. 'I thought he'd be rapt.'

'It's probably because of Grace,' Izram said.

'What d'you mean?'

'I reckon she's his girlfriend. That's why he doesn't want to leave her and go to Melbourne.'

Lan stared at him. 'His *girlfriend*? He's too old for Grace.'

'Plenty of women go for old guys. You see pictures of them in the magazines all the time. Look at that wrinkly Michael Douglas.'

Lan was unconvinced. Spinner was no film star. 'What makes you think she's his girlfriend?'

'She baked him a cake, didn't she? And she's been doing that for a long time, he said so. And she brought it round to him. They were sitting there together when we arrived. And they sat together at our Supporters' Dinner, remember. And he calls her WG.'

'That's because of some old cricketer. It's a nickname, so what?'

'Grown-ups — men and ladies — don't give each other nicknames unless they're in love,' Izram said.

Lan didn't know any grown-ups who were in love so he couldn't be sure about this piece of information, but Izram had an older sister who was always in love so perhaps he was right. 'What does Sheela call her boyfriend?' he asked, interested.

'The latest one? Possum Poo.'

Lan laughed incredulously. 'I'd sock anyone who called me Possum Poo.'

'You wouldn't if it was your girlfriend.'

'Would so. Anyway, I wouldn't have a girlfriend who called me a poxy name like Possum Poo. What does he call her?'

'Soppy names like Candyfloss and Honey Bunny.'

Yes, they were soppy all right, but at least they were sweet. Lan could see a romantic connection. But there was nothing remotely sweet about WG as a nickname.

He mused on this as he watched the net practice. The batsman had his shirt collar up and he was chewing gum and looking very cool. The bowler looked hot and rumpled. He did a full run up, walking a few paces, starting to jog, then building up speed. It was smooth, beautiful to see. The ball was forward in his hands, nice and loose. He let it fly, a lovely yorker that completely foxed the batsman. Lan felt like clapping. Batting might be more glamorous but where would cricket be without bowlers?

But then he thought of something. Spinner was a cricketer. And Grace was a cricket fan. Of course he'd give her a cricketing nickname: didn't he have one himself? Izram might be on to something.

'When you asked her why he didn't want to go

to Melbourne, she said it was something personal,' Izram reminded him. 'What else could it be?'

And she'd reached out and squeezed Spinner's hand, Lan now recalled. 'Even if you're right,' he said, 'so what? Grace wanted him to go to Melbourne. She's going to persuade him to go.'

'Melbourne's not the problem,' Izram said gloomily. 'It's afterwards.'

'What d'you mean, afterwards?'

'If they get married, things will change. We'll be lucky if he coaches us once a week. Wives don't like their husbands spending all their spare time playing sport. They want them home, mowing the lawn and cleaning the gutters and everything. And girlfriends are the same. They always want you to go out and do things with them, like shopping.'

Izram's argument carried the conviction of first-hand observation, but Lan wasn't persuaded. 'Grace is different. She likes cricket. And she supports the Nips.'

Izram conceded that it might make a difference.

'And it'll be good for him to get married,' Lan said. 'It must be lonely living on your own.'

'He's not alone, he's got Larri.'

'Yeah, that's true.' How could anyone be lonely with a wicked little dog like Larri? 'But he still needs someone to look after him and wash his clothes and see he eats the right food and all that.' Lan thought of all the things his mother did. How would they get on without her?

'I s'pose,' Izram agreed. 'If Spinner has to get married or have a girlfriend, Grace is as good as we'll get.'

Three

On the first day of the new year Lan hung one of his father's calendars (*Nguyen's Quality Fruit & Veg, 6 days to 7 p.m.*) on his bedroom wall next to his Shane Warne poster, and looked at it critically. The picture above the months was of four cute grey and white kittens tumbling out of a beribboned straw hat. His mother and the twins liked it but Lan thought it was dumb. What had kittens to do with fruit and vegetables? He wasn't a millionaire, his father grumbled; he had to buy stock calendars in bulk and the only choice this year had been between kittens or a puppy in a flowerpot.

Something more inspiring was called for, Lan decided. He rummaged in the plastic milk crate under his desk. Both the Melbourne Tourist Board and the Melbourne Cricket Club had generously responded to his email request and had sent him a stack of exciting glossy brochures and booklets. He flicked through them until he found a large colour photograph of the MCG. He cut it out and stuck it over the kittens in the hat. Now, where were those photographs that Izzie had taken of him and his bat on Boxing Day?

Izram had received a camera for Christmas and Lan, much to his joy and astonishment, had been given a cricket bat. Not being Christian, neither the Nguyen nor the Hussein family really celebrated Christmas, but it was hard to ignore the commercial pressure entirely. As Mr Nguyen had observed at the conclusion of the King's match, 'We are all turning Australian.'

As a photographer Izram still had a lot to learn, particularly when it came to focus and composition. With a pair of scissors, Lan carefully cut away the garage wall and the line of flapping washing in the background of the best photo, applied the gluestick and triumphantly stuck himself and his bat right in the middle of the MCG. Now that was an inspirational calendar!

There was a tap on the door and his father came in. 'Check it out,' Lan said, pointing.

His father looked at the newly-doctored calendar and gave a small start.

'That's me at the MCG. The Melbourne Cricket Ground,' Lan explained.

'Yes, I guessed that. Will you play there in Melbourne?'

'Well, no,' Lan admitted. 'All the matches are held at some school sports ground. But I might one day, when I'm a professional cricketer.'

Mr Nguyen responded with a sound that fell somewhere between an encouraging 'Mmm' and a sceptical 'Hmm'. It could mean 'Good luck, I'm sure you'll achieve your ambition.' Equally, it could mean, 'Not if I have anything to do with it.' Lan was well aware that even if his father's attitude towards sport had softened in the last few months, he still ranked school and study number one. And playing cricket was definitely not his idea of a professional career.

'It still shows the shop name,' Lan pointed out. 'But now there's a connection.'

'A connection?'

'Between the business and the picture, see? The message of that calendar is, eat plenty of fruit and vegetables if you want to be a champion.' Lan's eyes flicked to the poster of Shane Warne, living proof that one could also become a champion on a diet of pies, baked beans and pizza, but luckily his father wouldn't be aware of that.

'Ah!' His father hit his forehead, remembering what he'd come for. 'A phone call for you. A teacher.'

'A teacher? Which one?' Why was a teacher ringing him in the holidays?

'Mr Tissleton. Quick. Don't keep him waiting.'

Lan hurried into the kitchen and picked up the receiver. 'Hello?'

'Ah, Lan. Reg Thistleton here. You had a happy Christmas, I trust? You're enjoying the holidays?'

'Yeah. Thanks. I got a cricket bat.'

'Splendid! Cricket is why I'm ringing, as a matter of fact. Everything organised for the Melbourne trip?'

Lan knew the details by heart. 'Yeah, pretty much. We're leaving on the Overland on Thursday morning, January 18th, and the train trip takes the whole day and we arrive in Melbourne at eight o'clock that night. Somebody from the ACB meets us and we're staying in a school boarding house … Oh, you know that, don't you? Um, there's matches and stuff and some sightseeing and a coaching clinic and we leave again on the Overland on Sunday night and get back early the next morning. '

'Good show! Mr McGinty's going with you, I take it?'

'Yes, sir.' Grace had fulfilled her promise.

'Any parents going?'

'Um, we're not sure yet. Most of them have to work.'

'That's what I thought. Hence my call. The fact is, Lan, I'm off to Melbourne about that time. Family visit, staying with my daughter. Anyway, to get to the point, I'd be happy to help chaperone.'

'Chaperone, sir?' Lan didn't know the word.

'Supervise, keep an eye on you boys, particularly on the train. Departures and arrivals, always a worry, and it's a long trip. Can't leave it all to an old chap like Mr McGinty. What do you think?'

What Lan thought was that Mr Thistleton was an old chap too, perhaps not quite as old as Spinner but still old. Would two old men be better than one? He might need to get two wheelchairs. It would mean double the responsibility for him. But they could keep each other company and chat about cricket in the olden days. And the parents would be relieved.

'That'd be great, Mr Thistleton. D'you want me to send you the details?'

'No need for that. I'll follow it up. Well, goodbye, Lan. Happy New Year.'

'Happy New Year, sir.'

And why wouldn't it be happy?, Lan thought, putting down the phone. Starting high school was heaps scary, but going to Melbourne and winning the Harmony Cup would be a killer beginning to the year. Which reminded him: as captain, there were one or two things he needed to discuss with Spinner at practice on Thursday. But nothing major. Everything was on track for success.

'Don't play against the ball, Andy, hit with it! … Watch the ball, Lan! Keep yer eyes on it all the way to the bat … Slips, concentrate on the game. Anticipate where the ball's goin'. Expect that every single ball is comin' your way.'

Oh, it was good to get back in training. It was good to heave a ball and hit it with a bat. It was good to watch the matches on TV and then come out to Denby Reserve and play a game that was as much a part of the summer as the sunshine. Was there a more satisfying feeling in the world than watching a cricket ball speed along the ground after you'd whacked it right in the middle of the bat? Not unless it was dismissing a batsman with a wicked delivery that drifted in the air, skidded through and smashed the wicket.

Playing cricket was so exciting Lan wanted to do it every day. Especially now that he had his own bat.

'What can I do on my own?' he asked Spinner, at the end of the session. He flopped down on the grass and rummaged in his bag for his pen and notebook. 'You know, in between team practice and when I can't get to the nets?'

'Didya try the ball-in-an-old-sock routine?'

Lan nodded. Well, not an *old* sock. He'd taken one of his father's, which hadn't gone down well, but it was longer and stretchier than any of his. He'd put a ball in it and then tied it on a rope to the clothesline. It hung about ten centimetres from the ground and was good for practising forward and backward defence. Of course, after he'd belted it for an hour or so the sock was a lot longer and stretchier, which was what had caused all the fuss. But his mother had since donated some of her old panty hose and that was even better.

'What else?'

'Get a skipping rope,' Spinner advised. 'Skipping makes you light on your feet.'

Lan looked round at the others who were sitting or lying stretched out on the grass around him. Even Larri looked a bit flattened by the heat. 'Did you hear that? Skipping.'

'A bit girly, isn't it?' Andy said. 'My sister skips.'

'Boxers skip,' said Spinner, which settled it.

'What else should we do?' Lan asked, pen poised.

'Well, you c'n draw a set of stumps against a wall and bowl at that. You c'n always practise your fielding. Find a wall or a fence to throw a ball against, the rougher the better. Then the ball flies back at unpredictable angles.'

'OK. What else?'

'Keep fit. Run. Then run some more. When you feel buggered, run some more.'

Lan wiped the sweat from his brow and noted it in his book. He jotted down 'buggered' too. It was a useful word. 'OK. Maybe we should come early to practice and do some extra laps. What else?'

Izram, not at all enthusiastic about extra laps, could see signs of impending mutiny on the faces of some of the other Nips. He tugged at Lan's T-shirt and murmured, 'We're not playing for the Ashes, y'know. Give us a break.'

There were a few murmurs of agreement. 'We're on holidays,' Sal said.

'It's hot,' said Jemal, fanning himself with his hat.

Lan couldn't believe it. Here they were, about to compete in a prestigious interstate carnival, and whining about the heat and a little extra practice. What was that compared to national triumph? What had happened to the fighting spirit of Nips XI?

What would Steve Waugh say to a team like this?

Before he could say anything, Spinner patted him on the shoulder, letting his fingers linger and grip just tightly enough to serve as a warning. 'Want to know the best thing you can do right now, matey? Just enjoy your cricket.'

'I do,' Lan assured him. 'But I want us to get better and better and win this Cup.'

Izram, feeling disloyal for not supporting his captain earlier, nodded. 'If we're going all that way, we want to win.'

'We can't win if we're all dead of heat stroke,' Andy said.

'Andy's got a point,' Lan said suddenly. 'Spinner, I was going to ask you about acclimatisation.'

'Acclimatisation?' Spinner scratched his chin. 'What's that got to do with the price of eggs?'

Lan shook his head. 'It's nothing to do with eggs,' he explained patiently. 'It means that when you go to play in another country where the climate's different, it's a good idea to get there a bit early so you can get used to the different conditions. That's what the Aussies do when they go to India or Sri Lanka.'

'Or Pakistan,' Izram said.

'So I was wondering if we should go to Melbourne a few days early,' Lan went on. 'I mean,

I know the tickets have been bought and all that, but we could change them.'

Spinner looked puzzled. 'I'm not with ya. Melbourne's not Karachi or Colombo. We're not likely to cop a burst of hot steamy weather. And as far as me memory stretches, the water's safe to drink.'

'That's it. Water,' Lan exclaimed. 'It rains heaps in Melbourne and it's always cold, even in January. It's a well-known fact. We've never played in the cold and the wet. Maybe we oughta go over a few days before so we can get used to it.'

Spinner spluttered a bit, and groped in his pocket for a handkerchief. He didn't have one. He wiped his eyes on the back of his hand instead. 'You've been readin' too many cricketers' diaries,' he said.

Now it was Lan's turn to look puzzled. 'No I haven't. I read about it in the newspaper. How would I get to read someone's diary?'

'Because they publish them, matey. Every cricketer and his dog writes a book these days — or gets some scribe to write a book for him, more like. Captains write diaries and tour logs, umpires write their memoirs. Sometimes I think every bloke on the pitch is scribblin' away. Beats me how anyone has time to play cricket.'

So captains wrote tour diaries. Lan filed this

bit of information away and made a mental note to ask Grace which ones were worth reading. In fact, he might wander over to the library, now that practice was over. There wasn't much time with departure day just a week and a half away.

'Want to come to the library with me?' he asked Izram.

Izram shook his head. 'Nah. Some of us thought we'd go to the pool. What about coming too?'

The thought almost shocked Lan. Go swimming when there were scarcely enough hours in the day to practise his skills?

'You can have too much cricket, you know,' Izram said. 'Can't you, Spinner?'

'You c'n have too much coachin'. Don't know how much cricket is too much if ya love the game.'

Lan was pleased that Spinner had taken his side.

'Bet David's not slogging away in the nets,' Andy said.

'He doesn't have to,' Hiroki said.

'No, he's on *holiday*,' said Sal, still looking aggrieved.

David Ho was in Hong Kong, on a family visit. He was due back next week but Lan had no worries about his game. If Andy and Sal played cricket as well as David, they could go to the pool every day with his blessing. A captain thanked his lucky stars if he had a David Ho in his team.

'Well, who's coming to the pool?' asked Izram.

Spinner got to his feet and readjusted his battered Akubra. Instantly, the little fox terrier was on his feet too, alert for any proposed activity. 'Reckon I'll go with Lan to the library. Haven't read the papers today and it's cool in there. C'mon, Larri.'

Izram nudged Lan in the ribs. 'Grace,' he murmured. 'Told you so.'

Four

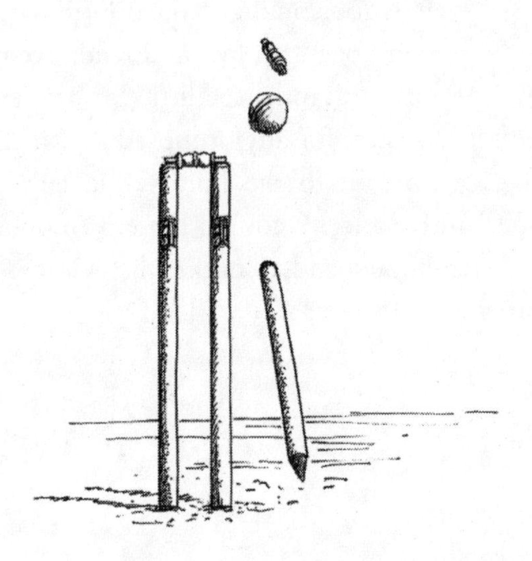

Lan clutched the telephone, aghast. David might be brilliant at delivering a ball to the boundary but he had no idea how to deliver bad news. He should have eased into it, perhaps talked about the weather for a bit, then given him a warning and asked if he was sitting down. For a moment he couldn't speak.

'Lan, are you there? Listen, I'm really sorry. I know what this means to the team.'

Could it possibly be David's idea of a joke? Perhaps in Hong Kong it was a New Year custom to play outrageous tricks on your friends. Sort of like April Fool, but in January.

'Jeez, David.'

'Bad timing, I know.'

'You're not kidding. The carnival's next week.'

'I didn't break my arm on purpose.' David sounded a little aggrieved.

Lan took a deep breath and tried to think. 'You definitely can't play then?'

'Do you know any one-armed batsmen?'

'Can't you have a cortisone injection or something?'

'Lan, the arm's in a cast! Anyway, we won't be coming back now until the nineteenth. I'm sorry, I really wanted to play, you know that. Tell the guys I'm sorry and wish them luck.'

No, it wasn't a cruel joke. David was too apologetic. 'How will I replace you?' Lan said despairingly.

'Put in Rikki and move everybody else up.'

Lan grunted. There wasn't much else he could do at this late stage. But Rikki Koh wasn't an all-rounder like David and he certainly couldn't bat with David's hard-hitting brilliance. He couldn't stride to the crease like David, collar up, casual but supremely confident, convincing the apprehensive bowler he was in for a hiding. Actually, there weren't too many in the team who could. To be certain of winning in Melbourne, they needed another David.

'You'll be OK,' David said. 'The team's got some good players. Hang in there.'

They said goodbye and a despondent Lan rang Izram and told him the bad news.

'Bummer,' said Izram. 'What are you gonna do?'

Izram's use of the singular pronoun reminded him that he was the captain and captains were supposed to be cool in a crisis and decisive. What was he going to do?

'Find a replacement,' he said. 'We can't just rely on Rikki. We need someone at least as good as David.'

'Bit late, isn't it?'

'State and Test teams make last-minute substitutions.'

'Yeah, but they have a lot of players to choose from,' Izram pointed out. 'We don't.'

'We can always —'

'Plus,' said Izram, 'we need a nip.'

Lan paused. 'Will that matter?'

'I reckon. This carnival's all about cultural diversity, remember. That's why we're invited, 'cos we're an ethnic team. The King's XI didn't get invited, did they?'

He was surely right, Lan thought. Which didn't make it any easier. Where in the next few days was he going to find an Asian-Australian batsman of the right age who could also bowl and field like a demon and who'd be free to travel to Melbourne next week?

'OK, let's think for a sec.' Somewhere in Izram's house a radio or TV programme blared. 'There's nobody at school or they'd be in our team already. There could be a player at Illaba High. Mr Thistleton might know someone to ask.'

'It's the holidays. The school's closed,' Izram reminded him.

'Mr Burrie at the cricket club knows all the local players.'

'He didn't know any nips when we were trying to put our team together, did he?'

'Well, you think of something then,' Lan said.

'We could put an ad in the paper. You know, like we were gonna do for a coach.'

'Costs too much.'

'Stick a notice up in the library then. It got us Spinner.'

'Not enough time. It might be up for days before anyone saw it.'

Izram said something which Lan didn't catch. 'What? I can't hear you. Your telly's too loud.'

'It's the radio,' Izram said. 'Mum likes to listen to talkback when she does the ironing. Hang on, I'll shut the door.'

Talkback radio. Of course! Thousands of people listened to that, didn't they? It was easy enough to get on: you just rang the talkback number and bingo, you were chatting live to the announcer. It didn't have to be a heavy topic like war in the Middle East or famine in Africa. People rang about all sorts of things: the state of the roads, the price of petrol, dead mice in loaves of bread, lost pets. Why not a call from someone urgently looking for a cricket player?

Izram came back. 'I've got an idea,' Lan said. He explained. 'I bet we find a replacement right away.'

'You have good ideas,' Izram said admiringly.

'Which station should I ring?' Lan asked.

They discussed the various programmes. In Izram's opinion, the talkback show his mother was currently engaged in listening to was not the right demographic. 'Old fogeys' radio,' was the way he put it.

'But the old fogeys might have kids,' Lan argued. 'I mean, your mother's listening, right? If she heard someone on air saying he desperately needed an under-14 Pakistani wicket-keeper for an interstate match, she'd tell you, wouldn't she?'

Izram admitted that on a good day and in the right mood, she might. 'But I reckon it'd be better to ring one of the drive shows. They talk a lot of sport on those, more than the morning programmes. So you're more likely to reach the right listeners.'

Lan yielded to Izram's superior knowledge of the media. 'I'll do it today. Which show?'

Izram recommended a show called 'On the

Ball with KC'. 'It starts at four o'clock. Hold on, I'll look up the number.'

'Casey who?'

'Not Casey, K-ay C-ee.'

'Just the initials?'

'Yeah.'

'What do they stand for? What's his name?'

'I dunno. It's not important. Just call him KC when you speak to him. Say it's a fantastic show and you listen every day.' Izram had some more good advice. 'Turn off your radio before you speak to him or you'll hear yourself and get muddled. Keep it short, he'll cut you off if you rave on. He's the only one allowed to rave. And keep repeating your phone number 'cos people never get it the first time.'

For the rest of the afternoon, Lan barricaded himself in his bedroom and rehearsed for his talk-back debut. 'Who you talking to?' Linh demanded, banging on his closed door.

'Nobody. Go away!'

'You talking to yourself?'

'Yeah.'

'I can hear someone else.'

What she could hear was Lan assuming a deep voice and pretending to be KC. *Well, Lan, a tough position for any skipper to find himself in so close to a demanding Cup match, but you sound just the man to lead your team to victory …*

'I'm acting,' Lan said.

'Like on TV?'

'Sort of.'

'Can I play too? I can act. I can be a Wiggles.'

'I'm a Wiggles too!' yelled Tien, joining the act. They both giggled and banged on the door.

Lan groaned and looked at his watch. When four o'clock came around, he had to make sure those two were busy elsewhere. How professional would he sound with the twins warbling Wiggles songs in the background?

At four o'clock he decided it would be a good move to listen to some of the show before he rang. He switched on his clock radio, found the station, and settled back on his bed. After fifteen minutes his head was spinning. 'On the Ball with KC' was a fast-paced mix of sports bulletins, listener calls, studio guests, discussion of matches played, discussion of matches yet to be played, arguments about results and players, and rapid-fire opinions from the host. An umpire's decision was 'absolutely appalling'; a caller who complained that on-field sledging was unAustralian and getting out of hand was 'an absolute wanker'; conditions at one ground were 'an absolute disgrace' but the game had been 'an absolute cracker'. When asked a question, people didn't say 'Yes', they said 'Most definitely,' or 'That's exactly right.' KC, who seemed to find a lot of things 'unbelievable', spoke quickly in a language that didn't always sound like English, and he had a habit of swallowing his consonants. Lan had difficulty keeping up with it all but at the same time he found the show strangely compelling.

The phone in the kitchen rang and he came out of his semi-trance and raced to answer it. It was Izram.

'Why are you answering the phone, you wacko?' Izram demanded.

''Cos you rang me, you dicko.'

'You oughta be on the phone to KC.'

'I was listening to him. Sort of getting a feel for the show first.'

'Ring him now! It might take a long time to get through.'

'OK, OK!'

Lan checked on the twins. They were in front of the TV watching the singing bananas. He punched out KC's number. A female voice answered, 'On the Ball with KC!' Lan said he'd like to speak to KC.

'What is your name, please?'

'Lan.'

'And what is your call about, Len?'

'Um, that's Lan.' He started to explain about the carnival. Before he was halfway finished, she interrupted.

'OK, that's fine. What was your name again?'

'Lan.'

'Can you spell that?'

Lan did. How difficult was L-a-n?

'And how old are you, Lan?'

He told her. Did they ask all callers their age? How old was KC?

'And your phone number? … Right, I'm putting you on after this segment, Lan. Please wait.'

Well, that was easy enough. And she was putting him on right away. Lan could hear the programme through the phone. A caller was suggesting that Sri Lankan sledging was worse because they spoke 'in their language' and did it on the sly. 'At least the Aussies get it out in the open,' said KC. 'Point taken.' Then came the ads, lots of them.

'And a young listener called Len has called. G'day, Len. Welcome to the show.'

With a jolt, Lan realised KC was talking to him. 'Um, g'day,' he said. 'Actually, my name's Lan. Am I on now?'

'You sure are. On the Ball with KC. Lan, is it? Lan, I understan' you're a member of a priddy unusual criggit team.'

'Well, we're all nips, if that's what you mean. Sal's really a wog, but he's an honorary nip.'

'That's, ah, Asian-Austrayans. You're Vietnamese, right?'

'Australian,' Lan said. 'But my parents come from Vietnam.'

'And the others?'

Lan gave brief details and explained how the team had got together.

'Goodonya! And now you've had a priddy excitin' invitation from the Austrayan Criggit Board. Tell us about that.'

Lan explained about the carnival in Melbourne and the Harmony Cup.

'Sounds like the sorta shot in the arm Austrayan criggit needs to propel it into the future, I reckon.'

'The thing is, our best batsman just broke his arm.'

'So you're castin' yer net far and wide for a subsitute?'

'A net?' Lan was momentarily confused.

'You've got a shoppin' list, right?'

Lan was even more confused. Did KC think he was going to Melbourne to *shop*? 'We need a batsman,' he said, 'so I thought maybe someone might be listening who —'

'OK, we're here to help! Any young criggiters listenin' out there who fit the bill, get on the blower right away and give Lan a call. What's ya number, Lan?'

Lan gave his phone number. Twice. He was

giving it again when he realised he'd been cut off. Apparently, that was the end of his innings.

The phone rang. It was Izram. 'Hey, that was pretty good. Wonder if anyone'll call?'

'If they do and if they sound OK, I thought I'd tell them to come along to the game on Saturday and we can see how they play.'

'You have good ideas,' Izram said.

Lan hung up, gratified. The phone rang. It was the first of many callers.

By five-thirty he was feeling desperate. Didn't anybody *listen*? He'd been very clear — or so he thought — but so far he'd heard from:

- a paraplegic who thought he was recruiting for wheelchair cricket;
- a Texan who didn't play cricket but thought he'd like to learn;
- someone selling lawn fertilizer;
- a woman who said the carnival was an appalling waste of government money;
- an insurance representative who tried to sell him a policy;
- a man who said cricket was an Aussie game and why didn't he go back to Vietnam?

The last call particularly depressed him. The caller had sounded so angry, as if he owned the game. And the country. When the phone rang again, Lan almost didn't answer. Then he sighed and picked it up.

'Hello.'

'Is that Lan? The guy who's looking for a batter?'

'Yeah.' At least the caller had got that right.

'I might be able to help you out.'

'Oh yeah.' No sense in showing any enthusiasm at this point.

'I'm the right age and I've been playing cricket almost three years now. I reckon I'm an attacking player, I bat third usually. I'm not bad at fielding and I'm an OK medium pace bowler. Oh, and I'm Chinese-Australian.'

'*Yeah?*' Lan brightened. This sounded more like it. 'D'you play in a team?'

'I did. At school last year. I've been thinking about maybe getting into club cricket this season.'

'Would you be able to come to Melbourne next week?'

'No problem.'

'Great. What are you doing this Saturday?' Lan gave the details of the match the Nips were playing at Illaba High. 'If you could show up, we might be able to give you a few hits and you can meet our coach and the other guys.'

'I can make it after eleven. If you need to get in touch with me, here's my number.'

Lan wrote it down. 'What's your name?'

'Sam. Chin Po. Just call me Sam.'

'OK, Sam. Seeya Saturday.'

Lan hung up, elated. He'd liked the sound of Sam's voice — strong and confident — and his no-nonsense approach.

The phone rang again. Who was it this time? A one-legged New Zealander? Someone offering him a credit card?

It was the producer of 'On the Ball with KC'. 'Congratulations, we've chosen you as the best caller of the day,' she said brightly. 'If you give me your address, we'd be pleased to send you out an executive floral arrangement.'

'A what?' Lan said, taken by surprise.

'A bunch of flowers.'

'Oh. Thanks, but …' An idea came to him. 'Can I send them to someone else? As a present?'

'If you like.'

'Great. Send them to Grace at the Illaba Library.'

'Just Grace?'

'Miss Grace, I guess.'

'Any message?'

'Message?'

'On the card that goes with them.'

'Oh.' Lan pondered. What did you write when you sent your girlfriend flowers? Didn't the flowers say it all? He couldn't put anything soppy; people in the library might see it and she'd be embarrassed. On the other hand, it ought to be a bit romantic.

'You still there?' said the producer.

'I'm thinking. What do most people put?'

'Depends. Congratulations, best wishes, compliments of the season, happy returns.'

'None of those seem right. It needs to be friendlier, but not too much.'

'Look, I haven't got all day, you know. What about "Thinking of you"?'

Lan didn't consider that very romantic. He'd been thinking of David most of the day but that didn't mean he was in love with him. On the other hand, the producer sounded as if she now rather regretted choosing him as the Caller of the Day so he had to come up with something quickly. What could he put? Thinking friendly thoughts of you? Thinking *very* friendly thoughts of you?

'*Hello?*'

'How about "With fond wishes"?' That seemed to strike the right note. 'Oh, and don't put my name on it, please,' he added quickly. 'Sign it Mystery Spinner.'

'Right. We'll see the flowers are delivered tomorrow morning.'

'Thanks.' Lan hung up the phone, well satisfied with his afternoon's work.

Five

Lan congratulated himself on his tactics. On its own, the bad news about David's broken arm would have demoralised the team. But he had given them the bad news and then immediately presented them with a solution. How could anyone not be impressed, both by the solution and his initiative in finding it?

'How many calls didya get after the radio show?' Andy asked.

'Heaps,' said Lan, 'but Sam was the best.' He managed to give the impression he had been auditioning eager batsmen all week.

'When do we get to see him play?'

'He'll be here later,' Lan said. 'I thought we might give him a few hits and see how he goes.'

The opposition, a second XI from North Illaba High, won the toss and elected to bat. Mr Thistleton, who was doing umpire duty, had arranged the match. 'They're a little older and more experienced,' he told the Nips, 'but that's all to the good. You won't improve unless you step out of your comfort zone.'

Which was probably true, thought Lan, but it would be nice to stay in the comfort zone long enough to actually get comfortable. These guys were a lot older and a lot more experienced. The batsmen were big and fearsome and smashed the balls as easily as if they were swatting flies. He didn't want to think about the bowlers.

By the end of the innings, the Nips were chasing a total of 159. In the absence of David, Izram was moved up to open the batting with Akram, but was bowled out for a mere seven runs.

Lan was batting next. He took off his hat and glasses, squinted at the sun and blinked several times, adjusting his eyes to the light. Think positive, he told himself. Today's going to be your day. It was something he muttered to himself like a mantra every time he walked to the crease. But would he ever not feel nervous walking to the crease? Please don't nick the first ball, he thought. Please let me get off the mark.

Izram came off and handed him the helmet. 'Good luck,' he said, 'you're gonna need it.' Which didn't help Lan's confidence. Neither did the sight of the huge bowler, champing at the bit to send down his next thunderbolt. Was that hair on his chest? Lan gulped, took guard and looked around the field.

The first delivery went flying past his nose. It was so close he swore afterwards he could see the whites of the kookaburra's eyes as the ball flashed by. Umpire Thistleton murmured a warning. The bowler grinned. Well, that was the first ball taken care of.

'Never be afraid of gettin' out,' Spinner had advised. 'The game's about scorin' runs and if you're doin' that you're puttin' pressure on the bowlers. Stay positive and play your shots.'

Lan calmed his nerves and played the shots but the runs came slowly, in singles and occasional twos rather than fours and sixes. He made twenty-seven before he was caught in the slips after a nicked delivery. He walked back to the benches, grateful he'd made that many but wishing he'd been able to stay in longer. It wasn't *essential* for the captain to do well but it certainly helped.

By the time Phon Phimonyanyong went in, victory looked remote.

Izram was unworried. 'It's only a game. We don't have to win every one.'

'Yes we do.' And we have to go in as if we know we can. That was now Lan's philosophy. That was *how* you won, by always believing you could and making the opposition fight for every run. It was something Phon and Andy and a few others in the team needed to learn. Even if you didn't win the game, there were your personal stats to consider.

'He's come on pretty good,' Spinner said, nodding at Phon. 'And he's a good runner between the wickets. See how he goes after the quick singles.'

Phon had been trying hard to improve his batting but Lan still wasn't ready to move him up any higher. 'What we need,' Lan said, 'is a big run scorer.'

He felt a light touch on his shoulder.

'Are you Lan Nguyen?'

He looked up, squinting against the sun. 'Yeah.'

'I'm Sam. Sorry I couldn't get here earlier.'

Was that spot-on timing or not? Lan marvelled. It had to be an omen. The very moment he had expressed a wish for a big run scorer Sam had appeared. Standing in front of him was a lithe athletic figure wearing dazzling whites and a soft-brimmed cricketing hat and clutching a sports bag.

Lan's first fleeting reaction was disappointment

that he wasn't bigger and taller, but he quickly reminded himself that skill had nothing to do with size. Hadn't he stood right behind Sachin Tendulkar at Adelaide Oval and marvelled that somebody so slight could produce so many mighty shots?

'Yeah, hi,' he said, 'I'm Lan.' Then he remembered that had already been established and, embarrassed, he hurried on. 'And this is Izram, our wicket-keeper, and Akram and Andy …' He introduced Sam to the players who were either sitting on the bench or in the near vicinity. 'And this is our coach, Mr Clarence McGinty.'

'I'm honoured to meet you,' said Sam. 'I'm very pleased to meet you, sir.'

He sounded so solemn that Lan fully expected him to bow, but he held out his hand instead and Spinner, looking slightly bemused, shook it. 'G'day, son. They tell me you want to join the Nips?'

'If they'll have me. If I'm good enough.'

'Now's yer chance to show us. Feel like goin' in next?'

Sam looked faintly alarmed, or as alarmed as somebody could look whose eyes were obscured by sunglasses. 'Don't worry,' Lan said quickly. He knew how he'd feel, thrown in as a tailender and expected to turn on the fireworks. 'We're chasing about seventy runs with one wicket and three overs left so we're not expecting miracles. I told the other captain one of our batsmen might be late.' He turned to Spinner. 'That's OK, isn't it? If we send in Sam instead of Rikki?'

'I wouldn't worry,' Spinner said. 'They'll never know the difference.'

Lan supposed he meant that in their whites and with a helmet on, everybody looked the same. But to his eyes there was something different about Sam and he wasn't sure he could put his finger on what it was. He considered it as Sam padded up.

Bang, down went the ninth wicket.

Phon walked off and Sam put on the helmet. Both of them were of similar height and build and both had light olive skin and straight black hair — Phon's soft and floppy and Sam's a little wilder and spikier. But as Sam walked to the crease, swinging his bat experimentally as he went, he looked way more professional than most of the Nips. Lan was suddenly reminded of something Spinner had told them early on: 'If you can't be a good cricketer, at least look like one.' At first Lan had assumed he was talking about wearing the proper clothing, but he'd come to realise it was much more than that. It was about confidence, fitness, technique — even the way you held your bat and stood at the crease.

That was it. That was what marked Sam out. He was staring at the bowler now, without flinching. He won't let anything rattle him, Lan thought.

The demon bowler sent down a rocket.

Lan just had time to think that if Sam didn't duck it would get him straight between the eyes when Sam hooked. He swung the bat around his shoulders in a splendid horizontal arc. The ball zoomed over the boundary.

'Wow,' exclaimed Izram. The Nips applauded wildly. What a beginning!

'He plays aggressively, right from the start,' said Spinner.

'I don't think I'd have hooked,' Lan said. 'Not on the first ball.'

'You worry too much, mate. At your level, it's all about hittin' the ball and scorin' runs and enjoying yourself. If the ball's there to be hit, then hit it. I'd sooner see someone get out attacking rather than defending any day.'

Sam sent the next one through mid-off. 'Hits the gaps too,' Spinner said approvingly.

The scattered spectators, who had either been half-asleep or packing up rugs and folding chairs in expectation of a quick end, sat down again and paid attention. Down at the other end, Satria Basalama suddenly looked like a rookie who unexpectedly and inexplicably had found himself partnering Don Bradman.

Sam stayed at the crease and let the singles go. The last ball of the over snicked the edge of the bat, just missed the leg stump and the wicket-keeper's glove and ran towards the boundary. Yelling 'Yes!', Sam exploded down the pitch, turning low and almost touching his hand to the ground.

'Blimey, he's a sprinter,' Spinner muttered.

Sam ran five lengths of the pitch before the ball was fielded and altogether clocked up a fast twenty-nine runs before Satria was run out and it was all over.

Lan, feeling mighty pleased, got to his feet. 'So, shall we sign him up for Melbourne, Spinner?'

'You could do a lot worse.'

Puzzled, Lan said, 'Why would I want a worse player?'

'You don't, matey. It's just an expression.'

'So "you could do a lot worse" really means "you couldn't do better"?'

Spinner scratched his chin. 'That's goin' a bit far. What it means is, "In the circumstances, considering all available options and weighing up the pros and cons, I strongly advise you to take positive action in this matter".'

'Right.' Satisfied, Lan went in with the others for the end-of-match courtesies.

'Bad luck, Satto,' he commiserated. He himself hated getting run out; it seemed such a wussy way to end your innings.

But Satria was nonplussed. As he saw it, his

role was to be the battler of the team, the one who struggled hardest and didn't give up. He was the one everybody could point to and say, If he can play cricket, so can I. Besides, thanks to the mystery batsman, he'd stayed in longer than he'd expected and some of the glory had surely fallen on him. His parents, who had been watching and who knew only slightly more about cricket than they did about quantum physics, seemed to think so too, and they rushed up to congratulate him.

Sam was still wearing his helmet. 'You were great,' Lan told him.

'I was a bit nervous,' Sam admitted.

'That bowler was hairy.'

'He didn't worry me. I decided long ago that I wasn't going to be scared of any bowler. I was just nervous I'd screw up and you'd choose someone else.'

Obviously, he hadn't realised how limited the options were. Lan longed to ask how he'd overcome his fear of fast bowlers but that could wait. 'You really want to go to Melbourne, don't you?' he said.

Sam shrugged. 'Who wouldn't? I mean, the Australian Cricket Board and all ...'

'Yeah. It's a big honour for the team.'

'Don't you want to check out my bowling?'

Lan knew he wanted Sam in the team even if he bowled like Minnie Mouse but he said, 'If you like. We can go in the nets for a while if you've got time. Did you come with anybody?'

'My sister drove me.' Sam gestured towards the cars parked at the edge of the playing field. 'But she'll wait.'

'Come and meet Mr Thistleton. He's a teacher, he's coming with us. He's got some papers and stuff about the trip. Your parents have to sign some of them.'

'My sister can do that,' Sam said. 'She's at university. I live with her.'

As they approached the benches, Mr Hussein came over. He thumped Lan on the back in his inimitable way. 'Bad luck, can't win them all, hey? But a jolly good finish. Who's the new batsman? I bet he's Pakistani!'

'This is Sam. He's Chinese.'

'You can't tell under that helmet. But you play like a Pakistani. Well done!' Mr Hussein thumped Sam on the back.

'My dad still thinks Pakistan leads the world in cricket,' Izram explained.

'We are up there on the top. Maybe not on the pinnacle but on the top,' proclaimed Mr Hussein with cheerful illogicality.

Sam took off his pads and only then took off the helmet.

'I'll take it.' Lan held out his hand.

For a brief moment as he handed it over, their eyes met — for the first time, Lan realised. Sam's were clear and brown but that wasn't surprising: everyone in the team had brown eyes. It was the expression in them as he looked straight at Lan that was the puzzle. What was it? Defiance? A challenge, certainly. *Well?* they signalled. *What do you think?* But hadn't Lan already told him? Then Sam, stooping, took his sunglasses from his bag and put them on.

Mr Thistleton came over and Lan introduced them.

'Splendid innings,' said Mr Thistleton. 'Can't have been easy, being sent in like that. Now, Lan tells me you'll be coming to Melbourne with us. A few formalities to go through. I've got a few papers here …'

It seemed to be decided. Everybody had been impressed by the newcomer's confident way with the bat and none of the Nips voiced any objections. Certainly not twelfth man Rikki Koh. Ever since David's accident, he'd been having recurrent nightmares about being pulverised to a powder at the MCG wicket in front of a jeering crowd. He was only too glad to get the trip without the trauma.

Sam went and got his sister and Lan and Izram met her briefly. She didn't say much beyond confessing an ignorance of cricket and Lan thought she seemed a little uncomfortable, as if she wanted the formalities over and done with so she could leave. But she listened politely to Mr Thistleton and took all the papers and permission slips and insurance forms and dietary sheets and assured him they would all be signed and Sam would be at the railway station on Thursday morning to depart with the Nips on the Overland to Melbourne.

'That's it, then,' Lan said to Izram in satisfaction. 'We're in with a chance. He'll be good on the team. And good *for* the team. Our batsmen need to attack more.'

'He's a bit serious,' Izram said.

'What d'you mean?'

'Just that he's a bit serious. He doesn't smile or crack jokes or kid around.'

'He doesn't know anyone! And he knew we were all watching him. How full of fun would you be? Anyway, what do we want, a batsman or a comedian?'

'What's his bowling like?'

'We're having a session in the nets. Come with us.'

'His sister doesn't look too keen.'

Lan glanced across to the car park. Sam and his sister seemed to be having a heated discussion. 'Maybe she doesn't want to wait,' he said. 'I don't s'pose it matters much. Our batting line-up's pretty strong.'

'You talk like a real cricketer now, you know that?'

'Do I? What's that mean?'

'When you first got the idea for the Nips you didn't know anything about cricket. Remember that first meeting we had?'

'Yeah.' Lan grinned. It seemed half a lifetime away. 'I've read a lot of cricket books and watched a lot of videos since then. Grace picks them out for me.'

He didn't tell Izram that he also kept a scrapbook under his mattress full of match reports, pictures, swap cards, and downloadings from the Web. Not to mention a pie bag personally autographed by Shane Warne. Lan kept it under his mattress not only to keep it unpolluted from the inquisitive hands of his mother and the twins but in the hope that good vibes or karma or whatever you called inspirational motivation would somehow drift upwards through the springs and fabric and into his brain as he slept.

'I was thinking of keeping a tour diary while we're away,' he said. 'You know, like Test captains do.'

'Good idea. I can take the photos. Oh, about Grace …' Izram lowered his voice. 'She and Spinner are having dinner at the Bukhara tonight. How romantic is that?'

'Is it?' Lan had never thought of the Bukhara as particularly romantic. But then, he was most often there after school when the tables were bare and Mr and Mrs Hussein were banging pots about in the kitchen.

'It looks different at night,' Izram said. 'There's candles and flowers and a blue spotlight behind the fish tank.'

Flowers, Lan remembered. That was why Grace and Spinner were dining together. He told Izram about the radio station and the flowers he'd sent her in Spinner's name.

'That's probably it,' Izram said. 'They've never been to the Bukhara together before.'

'Maybe he's getting ready to propose,' Lan said.

'He ought to do it before we go away. Just in case she meets someone else.'

'We'll only be away four days!'

'That's heaps of time. Sheela used to have this boyfriend called Stefan and he went away on a football training weekend and she went to a club with her girlfriends and met this other guy and when Stefan came back she dropped him. But if she'd had an engagement ring and everything she wouldn't have gone to the club and she wouldn't have met this other guy so it was Stefan's fault.'

Lan realised again that Izram knew far more about romance than he did. It must be very useful having an older sister. He wondered if Sam was similarly enlightened.

He rejoined them, having persuaded his sister to wait, and the three of them had a brief session in the nets with Spinner. Lan was secretly relieved to observe that Sam's bowling, while more than competent, wasn't quite as brilliant as his bowling. He wanted the best for the Nips, of course, but it would be a bit much to cope with if the newcomer to the team outclassed him at both batting *and* bowling.

Six

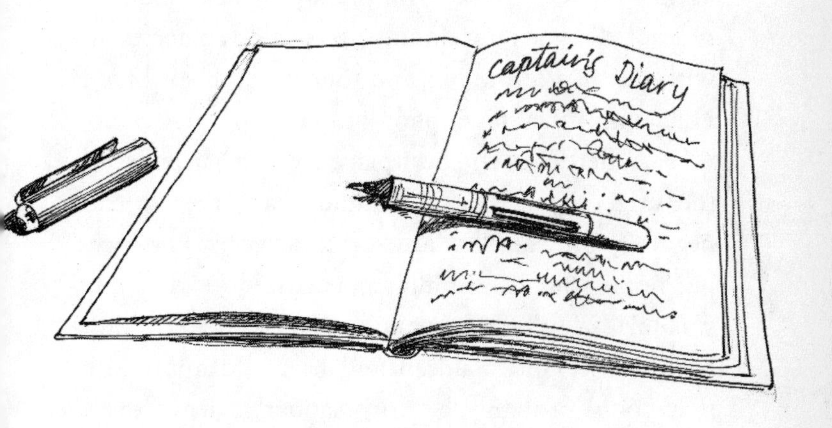

A tour diary of a completely unknown schoolboy cricketer did not hold quite the appeal of one penned by Australia's Test captain or the world's greatest spin bowler, Lan realised that. But one day he intended to be like them and it would be good to have one book under his belt when he was. Even if it was never published it would be a valuable historical document. Grace had offered to keep it safe for posterity at the Illaba Library.

But could this trip to Melbourne really be called a tour? Izram said it could. 'We have to cross a border, don't we? So going to Victoria's like going to a foreign place. Everything'll be different there.'

Lan bought a thick exercise book at the newsagency and covered it with pictures of his favourite players. They would do until he could replace them with pictures of the Nips on tour, courtesy of Izram Hussein, official team photographer.

Where was the best place to start? In most of the cricketing diaries Lan had read, the writers began by proclaiming how sad they were to be leaving home, but he couldn't honestly write that. He was thrilled to be leaving home. Of course, he didn't have a wife and children and he could appreciate that you'd probably be a lot sadder to leave them than your mum and dad. But he would try to strike the right note of regret. He noted, too, that Steve Waugh's diaries contained numerous details of meals (wait until his mother told him yet again that McDonald's would poison his insides, he'd tell her the touring Aussie Test team seemed to eat little else), and notes for the many inspirational pep talks he gave his players. Poems, too: Captain Waugh encouraged his men to motivate each other by writing inspirational verse. Lan wasn't sure how the Nips would react to such an idea, but it was sure to earn the approval of Mr Thistleton. Anyway, he'd try to make his touring diary just as interesting and professional as Steve's.

Captain's Diary Wednesday 17 January

This time tomorrow we will be on our way to Melbourne. If you're serious about cricket you have to tour. Many of us have never been away from our families before and of course it is also tough on those who are left behind. Mark Waugh says you have to be able to adjust and handle the pressures of the nomadic life or you won't survive, so it's a good thing I am starting young. OK, it is not the same as touring India or Pakistan, but we will be away from home and we will have to cope with strange food and water (I hope everyone stays healthy), not to mention the climate and accommodation. (We are staying at a school. Andy says there will be iron beds and bars on the window.)

Thursday 18 January

Today was sad for my mother. When the time came to go to the station she bravely choked back her tears and made me promise to change my underwear every day. She has made me two new cricket shirts. She also made me take a huge plastic lunch box full of food, even though I told her you could get food on the train. She said train food was poison, and did I want to start my national cricketing career with diarrhoea? My father also looked sad as he said his final goodbye. He told me to behave honourably and not to do anything to disgrace the Vietnamese people. I would be representing them, he said. This is a scary thought as I have never represented anybody before, let alone a whole nation. Then he gave me some money! The twins looked sad, too. I warned them to stay out of my room and not to touch my stuff. They waved and waved, as if they knew they would not be seeing me again for a long time. I will never forget the look on their little faces.

When I met up with the team at the station I was really excited. I felt like I was starting a new chapter in my career. First North Illaba, and now the Nips are going national. It has been a fast track and I will have to perform well. The press were there to see us off and get some pictures and I held a press conference. We all posed in front of the Overland and then I had to stand on the steps and wave a cricket bat. I hope they don't use that photo: I felt like a dork.

Afterwards, the reporter interviewed me. It was an opportunity to share some final thoughts on what lay ahead. The reporter said, 'What do you think your chances are for the Cup?' and I said, 'Pretty good.' Then I said, 'We're looking forward to the challenges ahead,' which sounded very professional.

Lan nibbled the end of his pen and watched the gum trees and red roofs flash by outside the window. Well, perhaps one reporter and a photographer for the *Illaba Messenger* couldn't really be called a press conference. And a farewell at the railway station, however excited and emotional, didn't have quite the glamour of an airport departure. Test cricketers didn't depart the country clutching pillows and plastic lunch-boxes, for a start. But he *had* been interviewed. He looked at his watch and flipped to a new page.

'What are you writing?' Andy asked, leaning over the back of his seat. Lan told him about his tour diary. 'Nothing's happened yet,' Andy said.

'A lot's happened. Leaving home. The press conference. Now the flight — I mean, the train trip. Readers are interested in all that.'

'What readers?'

'Well, you know … if it's published one day. Cricket books sell heaps, especially books by captains.'

Andy conceded the truth of this. He peered at the open page of Lan's notebook. 'So what have you written?' He read out:

8.50 a.m. Boarded the Overland for trip to Melbourne. Found seats. I am next to Iz.
9.01 a.m. Train left for Melbourne.

'Not very exciting so far,' Andy said. 'You might have to beef it up a bit. You know, put some jokes and stuff in.'

'Not unless someone tells a joke,' Lan said. 'You don't just make things up. Everything in a diary is s'posed to have happened.'

'Then I'll tell a joke and you can put it in,' Andy said.

'Great. Thanks.' Lan nibbled his pen again. Should he put in anything about Spinner and Grace? Perhaps not, especially since Grace was going to be the diary's custodian. If they eventually got married, he could always add some details. At present, he wasn't sure what the state of play was.

'What happened at the Bukhara?' he asked Izram. 'Did Spinner and Grace turn up on Saturday night?'

Izram confirmed that they had.

'Were they all romantic?'

Izram wasn't sure. 'They talked a lot.'

'That's good. Did Grace say anything about my flowers?'

'Not to me, why would she? Anyway, they didn't stay long.'

'They could have been going on somewhere. Dancing, a club?' Lan had a hard time imagining Spinner dancing in a club but love did strange things to people, he knew that much.

'I don't think so. They didn't leave together. I mean, Grace's car was parked out the front and she got in and drove away and Spinner walked off. I s'pose he went home.'

That didn't sound good. 'Did they have a quarrel?' Lan asked.

Izram shrugged. 'Dunno. They might have had a quiet one that I didn't notice.'

'If they did, and he's away in Melbourne, anything might happen. Grace might find another boyfriend, like Sheela did.'

'Or he might find another girlfriend,' Izram said.

That seemed far less likely. 'Where's he going to find a girlfriend at a junior cricket carnival?' Lan said. 'We'll just have to keep reminding him how nice Grace is.'

Captain's Diary

We are in the Red Kangaroo Service. There are double seats that can tip back like airline seats, and they can swivel around so that four people can look at each other or play cards and games on a table that folds away against the wall. This is heaps better than a plane where you hardly have any space and have to look at the back of someone's head the whole trip. There are screens, too, so I hope that means videos as we have a lot of time to get through. We will travel 828 kilometres and the trip will take twelve and a half hours. Spinner says it used to take twelve and a half hours when he travelled in the train forty years ago so things haven't improved in the speed department, but the carriages are a lot swisher.

When we were all getting on at Adelaide he said to the man in uniform who was standing near the steps, 'Don't let the train go before we're all on board, will you, guard?', and the man said, 'I'm not a guard, I'm a Hospitality Attendant.' Spinner said in that case he'd have a beer but the Hospitality Attendant said he'd have to wait until the Lounge Car was open. (I thought a Hospitality Attendant would take care of people who didn't feel well or got train-sick, but Spinner said 'hospitality' meant being kind to strangers or guests.)

Then we were off and the feeling in the team was good right from the start. Everybody was excited and jumping up and down and swivelling their seats and pulling down tables and Mr Thistleton said 'Settle down, boys!' so many times I thought I was back in school! Later we started telling jokes. This was Andy's joke:

There's a knock at the front door. A man opens it and sees a snail sitting on the doorstep. He picks it up and throws it as far as he can. Three years later, there's a knock. The man opens the door and there's the same snail on the doorstep. It looks up and says, 'So what was that all about?'

I thought this was pretty funny. The snail had taken three years to crawl back but still thought the man would remember it. And it's funny because you don't expect snails to talk. Then we told all the 'knock-knock' jokes we could remember, and when we got to sixty-three some old people who were sitting in front of our group got up and grabbed all their things and moved further down the carriage, which was kind of them because then we could swing their seats around. Izram told a good cricket joke:

The class are having a spelling test and the teacher tells Akram to go to the black-board and write the word 'bowling'. Akram takes the chalk and writes: B-O-E-L-L-I-N and the teacher says, 'That's the worst spell of bowling I've ever seen.'

Everyone killed themselves laughing except Akka. (He is not a good speller.) Akka said he had a much funnier joke: There was this cricketer who goes to a doctor and says, 'Doctor, I feel terrible. I can't score runs, I can't hold a catch, I'm a rotten bowler, what can I do?', and the doctor says, 'Why not get another job?' and the cricketer says, 'I can't, I'm playing for Pakistan tomorrow.'

Iz didn't find this as funny as the rest of us, and for a moment it looked as if things might get a bit hairy. But Spinner said they used to tell the same joke when he was a boy except that the cricketer was playing for England, and this time we all laughed. Then suddenly a man who was sitting a couple of seats behind Spinner said loudly, 'Hey, I'm from England'. We all stopped laughing and looked at him, wondering if he was going to get mad or maybe call the Hospitality Attendant and complain. But then he sort of shrugged and said, 'OK, I suppose they are a pretty weak team.' Spinner said he would buy him a beer later to cheer him up.

Sam didn't tell any jokes. He has been a bit quiet, although I noticed him talking to

Spinner. I guess it's hard joining a team that has been together for as many months as we have. His sister brought him to the station. She gave me a card with her phone numbers on it and said, 'You're the captain. This is just in case'. I asked her, 'Just in case what?' and she said, 'Just in case anything.' So, like the snail, I don't know what that was all about.

At lunchtime we all went to the Lounge Car and bought pies and pasties so now I feel like a real Aussie cricketer on tour. I asked Spinner if he would like some of my mother's noodles and spring rolls and he said, 'Is the Pope Catholic? Hand 'em across, matey', so they weren't wasted.

When we came back to our seats, Sal said, 'Oh, guess what, we've got a team song.' Then he pulled a CD from his bag. It was by a group called Mental as Anything and one of the tracks was called 'The Nips Are Getting Bigger'. I couldn't believe it: someone had written a song about us! But Sal said no, it was written years and years ago.

We passed it around and we all had a listen and it was pretty good, but nobody could understand what it was about. We gave the headphones to Spinner and he listened to it and said it was about drinking rum. I said,

'But what does the singer mean, the nips are getting bigger? Is someone biting him?' Spinner explained that a nip was a little drink of spirits. If you poured a little bit of whisky or rum or brandy in a glass, that was called a nip. So if the nips were getting bigger, you were pouring more and drinking more and getting drunker.

Mr Thistleton said it sounded a *very* unsuitable song and we were not to sing it under any circumstances. But we all really liked the chorus — it just goes *Woah oh, the nips are getting bigger!* four times and in a really funky way — so after a bit he gave in and said, 'Oh, very well, just the chorus then.' So that's our new team song. We all practised *Woah oh, the nips are getting bigger!* over and over and over. It's fun to sing. The people who had moved right down to the end of the carriage then got up and headed towards the Lounge Car. I suppose the song made them feel thirsty.

I went and sat next to Sam for a while because it's the captain's duty to look after his players and make sure everyone is relaxed and happy. Also because he had a stack of cricketing magazines which looked interesting. Sam is interesting too when you get talking to him. He knows a lot about the game and like me he is very ambitious. I asked him how he started.

He said, 'I always liked sport. I only really go to school to play sport. Athletics, tennis, swimming.'

I said, 'Football?' and he said, 'No, not football. In junior primary we played muck-about cricket, then Super 8. Some of my friends got bored with cricket but I loved it, I always wanted to play.'

I said, 'Your parents don't mind?' and he sort of shrugged and said, 'They don't mind too much about me playing sport as long as it doesn't interfere with my studies. I'm not brilliant at school work like my sister.'

Then he asked me a lot of questions about the boarding school we were staying in and what the rooms and bathrooms and stuff would be like but I said I didn't know. He seemed a bit worried about sharing, especially since Spinner was snoring away across the aisle and sounding like a broken chainsaw, so I said I didn't think any of the Nips snored. (But I don't really know; maybe some of them do.)

Later Sam joined the others in some card games, which was good, and I talked to Spinner about team tactics, and we watched a video and went back to the Lounge Car again. Spinner and Mr T. have been to the Lounge Car heaps of times and haven't fallen down, even though it's not easy to walk on a train, so I don't think wheelchairs are going to be necessary. When we came back we told some more jokes and sang our team song again and I explained about writing poems for motivation, like Steve Waugh's men. Andy said, 'Here's one: Two, four, six, eight, We are the Nips and we are great.' I guess it's a start but it's not really a poem.

At last there came the welcome sight of Melbourne as the train pulled in just after 8 p.m. It had been a good trip but a long one and everyone in our carriage, especially the old people at the front, felt glad it was over.

It didn't look like the station on the brochure but Spinner said that was Flinders Street Station and this was Spencer Street. It was raining when we arrived and Spinner said, 'That proves we're in Melbourne.' But by the time we got out of the station and into the bus the rain had stopped.

Mr Thistleton said, 'Now <u>that</u> proves we're in Melbourne.'

I don't know why it does but I am very excited to be here.

Seven

Mr Thistleton's daughter was waiting for him on the platform and he departed with her, after making himself known to the young woman from the Australian Cricket Board. 'I'll catch up with you boys in due course,' he said. 'Best of luck in the matches tomorrow.'

The young woman was wearing a smart blazer with the ACB shield on the pocket. She led them along the platform to where a mini-bus was waiting. 'What a long trip you've had,' she said. She smiled at Tomas, who was trotting along beside her. 'You must be tired.'

'I'm buggered,' Tomas agreed.

Her smile faltered a little.

'He's picking up some Australian expressions,' Lan explained.

'Oh. Right. How many of you speak English?'

'We all speak English,' Lan said firmly. 'Some of us were even born here.'

'I just asked because that's not always the case in some of the other teams.' She smiled at him. Lan thought she was very pretty, as well as friendly. He wondered if she was a Hospitality Attendant.

Their bags were checked and loaded and then they all piled into the mini-bus. As they drove out of the station forecourt and into Spencer Street, the young woman addressed them.

'Hello, everyone. My name is Laura Jolly. Please call me Laura. I'm a Game Development Officer with the Australian Cricket Board and I'd like to welcome you to Melbourne.' Briefly, she recounted the Board's involvement in promoting cricket within indigenous and multicultural communities and told them about an indigenous cricket carnival she'd recently attended in Alice Springs. 'That really gave us the idea for the Harmony Cup. We've got teams from Darwin, Alice Springs, Queensland, Tasmania and the Tiwi Islands coming to Melbourne — in fact, they've already arrived — as well as teams very much like yours from here in

Melbourne. I'm sure we're going to have a great three days.'

She spoke with enthusiasm and Lan, who had been expecting a man, was a little surprised. Apart from Grace, he'd never met any female who had shown much interest in, let alone knowledge of, cricket. Thinking of Grace reminded him of his on-going mission. He turned around to Spinner, who was in the seat behind him, and said, 'Reckon Laura Jolly knows as much about cricket as Grace does, Spinner?'

'I'd be surprised. That woman's a walkin' Wisden.'

'A what?'

'A cricket encyclopaedia.'

'Yes, she is,' Lan agreed. 'Grace knows every-thing. She's very very smart.'

Spinner leaned forward and said in a low voice, 'Have a quiet word with young Tommy later. Explain to him that you don't go droppin' words like "buggered" when ladies are present.'

'OK. Are there any other words like that?'

'If I hear anyone usin' them, I'll let you know.'

'We'll take a little detour past the Melbourne Cricket Ground,' Laura announced. 'I guess you'd like to see the mighty MCG?'

'Is the Pope Catholic?' Lan and Izram chorused together, and everybody laughed.

It was still light outside and the recent shower of rain had refreshed the city. Lan pressed his face to the window, impressed by its architecture and vitality. So many glass towers and tall buildings, dazzling shop fronts and busy streets. So many people and cars and buses and trams!

'January's a quiet month,' Laura said, seeing his interest. She sounded almost apologetic. 'Lots of people take their holidays and go to the beach. Things will get a lot busier from next week.'

Busier? Lan was even more impressed.

'There it is!' Andy called out. 'There's the MCG!'

And there it was in the near distance, a huge stadium set among green parklands and surrounded by six gigantic light towers, the floodlights making it glow with promise in the soft summer evening. 'We call it "the G",' Laura said. 'The very first Test match was played there, in 1877.'

'Against who?' asked Akram.

'England, of course,' said Laura, smiling.

'I bet Australia won,' Lan said.

'We did. By forty-five runs.'

'Yay!'

Lan turned in his seat again. 'Is the G better than Adelaide Oval, Spinner?'

'It's bigger. They can get near on 100 000 punters in there.'

'But better?'

Spinner grunted. 'Better? What does better mean? All pitches are different.'

'We're hoping to fit in a tour during your stay,' Laura said. 'It's very interesting. You see the players' changing rooms and you even get to walk on the hallowed turf itself. Let's cross our fingers that the weather stays fine and we don't have interrupted play.'

Lan crossed his fingers immediately. After all his daydreams of glory at the MCG wicket, it would be so cool to actually see it for himself and put his foot on the hallowed turf. Spinner had used that expression too. 'It's a sacred site,' he'd said. 'Sacred to millions of players and sports fans. A place where the tribes gather and worship.'

'Like a church or a temple?' Lan had asked.

'To Melburnians, it's a cathedral.'

Seeing it now, Lan didn't think it looked anything like a cathedral, but the illuminations made it glow in a sort of holy way and he imagined that thousands of prayers must have been murmured within its walls. *Please God, let my team win. Please God, let me score a century today. Please God, don't let me get out first ball.* If he did get to step on the hallowed turf he'd secretly scoop up a bit of it and take it home and keep it with the other treasures under his bed. His mother had a little bottle filled with earth from her old home in Saigon which she kept by the shrine next to Grandma Mai's photograph.

They drove through a suburb which Laura told them was called Kew. Lan wrote 'Queue' in his notebook and thought it a funny name for a suburb, not to mention a confusing one. Suppose you were walking along and suddenly came across a sign saying 'Queue', or even 'Post Office Queue' or 'Shopping Centre Queue'? You might start to line up.

'This is St Paul's,' Laura announced, as the bus turned and drove through big decorative iron gates. 'The school's closed for the summer holidays, of course, but you'll be staying in the boarding house.'

They drove along a long tree-lined driveway and past tennis courts and playing fields that reminded Lan of King's College back home. Then the main school building, with its ivy-clad cloisters and clock tower, came into view. The bus pulled up outside a more modern, two-storey, red-brick building surrounded by lawns and garden. 'Here we are!' Laura said brightly. 'Get out and stretch your legs and I'll just go and see who's about.'

Spinner made them unload the bags instead and soon Laura came back with a rather harassed-looking young man she introduced as Mr Warton, a boarding-house master who would be on hand during their stay to keep an eye on them and make sure things ran smoothly. 'I'll say goodbye now,' she said. 'I'll be back tomorrow at 8.30 with a bus to take you all to Bulleen, where the matches will be played.'

Mr Warton helped them carry the bags into the entrance hall. 'We'll get the rooms sorted out later but the main thing now is to get you all fed,' he said, looking as worried as if a whole trainload of refugees had been dumped on his doorstep without notice. 'The other boys have already eaten of course — dinner is served at six-thirty — but you'll meet everyone at breakfast tomorrow. So, this way to the dining room!'

'I'm starving,' Izram muttered, the meat pie, sausage roll, bag of crisps and ice-cream he'd consumed just a few hours ago now just a distant memory.

They were shown into a pleasant, if functional, room containing several long tables, two of which had been set up for them, and a servery at one end. 'Help yourself to the food,' said Mr Warton. 'I hope it's satisfactory. We've tried to be multicultural.' Aside to Spinner he murmured, 'We do our best to provide a balanced diet in line with individual preferences but it's not always possible. The important thing is to make sure there's suffi-cient *quantity* for healthy appetites, don't you agree?'

Spinner agreed that was indeed the important thing and assured Mr Warton they all had healthy appetites.

There was a choice of two rice and noodle dishes and stir-fry vegetables, and afterwards, fruit salad and cream, and a sort of pale wobbly custard shape that everybody but Spinner ignored. After they had eaten, Mr Warton, looking worried, said he knew they were tired but he had a few announcements which he would try to keep short.

Lan, who up to that point hadn't felt tired at all, suddenly realised that he was, even though he hadn't done much all day except sit on a train. But of course he had been up since practically dawn. Then Mr Warton reminded them to advance their watches thirty minutes because they were in Victoria, and suddenly it was almost ten o'clock instead of not quite nine-thirty so it was really no wonder he felt tired.

'Breakfast and dinner will be served here in the dining hall,' Mr Warton continued. 'We suggest you rise about 7.15 in time for breakfast at 7.40. Following breakfast, there's time to gather equipment and so forth before the bus comes at 8.30. Lunch will be at the pavilion at Bulleen, and you return here for dinner at 6.30. Lights out are normally at 9.30, but of course we've made an exception tonight.'

'It's like being back at school,' Andy muttered.

'We *are* in school,' Sal said.

'Yeah, but not our school. And it's holidays.'

'We're on tour, and we're here to play cricket,' Lan reminded him. 'We have to be disciplined.'

'Lighten up,' Andy said.

Sam threw Lan a sympathetic look and he was grateful that one person at least appreciated that as captain he had certain responsibilities.

Mr Warton hadn't finished. 'The rooms upstairs accommodate four each, so there are three put aside for your team. Plus, of course, a room for … er, Mr McGinty. I hope that's satisfactory? So if everyone will follow me … Collect your bags as we go through.'

As they arrived at the landing at the top of the stairs, Spinner pulled a piece of paper from his pocket. 'Right, listen to me. Your captain and yours truly have drawn up a room list which we arrived at after a long consultation and by a highly scientific method. Namely, puttin' all yer names in me 'at and drawing them out again.' Lan knew this wasn't strictly true. They'd juggled a few. 'So we want no arguments now,' Spinner continued. 'You got a problem, see Lan tomorrow.' He put on his glasses. 'Right, room one: Satto, Rikki, Jemal, Phon. Room two: Andy, Sal, Hiroki, Akka. Room three: Tom, Sam, Izzy, Lan. You've got ten minutes to unpack, wash up and get into bed.'

They were shown their rooms, which were large with windows overlooking the garden and four single beds, not iron bunks, as Andy had predicted. The plaid bedcovers matched the curtains and the pinboards over the desks still displayed posters left by departing boarders. Lan took the bed nearest the door and found himself gazing into the kohl-rimmed eyes of Britney Spears. Izram took the bed opposite him, while Sam and Tomas were in the other corners. A door between their two beds led into an en-suite bathroom.

'Hey, this is pretty cool,' Izram said. 'I wouldn't mind going to boarding school.'

'How you doing, Onya? Everything OK?' asked Lan, who thought his youngest player might be feeling a little homesick. But Tomas, whose long list of temporary accommodations had included trucks, shelters, a refugee camp, a ship's cabin, migrant hostels and crowded council flats, had left homesickness behind him long ago. This was wonderful.

'Bewdy!' he said happily.

'Anyone want a quick shower before bed?' Lan asked.

'No, but I want the loo.' Sam grabbed something from his bag and disappeared into the bathroom, closing the door behind him.

'Hey wait, I want to clean my teeth.' Izram tried to follow him but the door was locked. He rattled the handle.

'Leave him alone,' Lan said.

'C'mon, there's four of us. What if we all went in one at a time?'

'He'll only be a couple of minutes. Your teeth won't drop out while you're waiting.'

They unpacked in silence and put their clothes away. When Sam emerged from the bathroom he was wearing blue and white striped pyjamas. 'It's all yours,' he said, and climbed into his bed. 'Good night.' He turned his back to them and pulled the bedclothes around his shoulders.

'Well, he's going to be fun to share with,' Izram muttered.

'He's tired. Everyone's tired.' Lan took his toilet bag and went into the bathroom.

Tomas followed him. 'I write poem for you, Lan. Like Steve Waugh.'

'Great.'

'In head now. On paper tomorrow.'

'T'rific, Onya.'

They were too tired to do more than clean their teeth, change and fall into bed. Lan felt a tension in the room. Perhaps Izram felt it too because he said moodily, 'It was raining when we arrived and now it's hot and sticky.'

'Put the overhead fan on then.'

Izram got out of bed and switched it on. There was silence for a while, except for the soft hum, and then Izram said in the darkness, 'Hope we wake up in time tomorrow. That Warton guy is a real control freak.'

On the point of dozing off, Lan was jolted back into full wakefulness. Was it his job to get everybody up in time? And if so, who would wake him? 'I'd better check with Spinner,' he said. He clicked on his light and got out of bed.

The coach had been allocated a double room to himself along and on the opposite side of the corridor. The door was ajar and the light on. Lan tapped and peered in. Spinner wasn't there, but the contents of an ancient canvas carry bag had been tipped out in a messy pile onto one of the beds — obviously Spinner's idea of unpacking. The adjoining bathroom was in darkness.

Then Lan heard his voice. He followed it, padding along on his bare feet, and came to a wide landing where the corridor met the back staircase. There were chairs and a hall table and a blue public phone on the wall, and Spinner was standing with his back to the corridor, speaking into it.

Lan drew back and waited for him to finish. He had a sheet of paper in his hand which looked like a letter, and the conversation seemed to be about tomorrow's activities because Lan picked up the words 'Bulleen playing fields' and 'about eight-thirty'. Wasn't it a bit late at night to be ringing people about cricket? There was a pause and then Spinner said something about water under the bridge and how it had been a long time, and his voice didn't sound the same as it did when he spoke to the Nips.

Lan shuffled his feet a bit and Spinner turned round and saw him. He looked rather like the twins did when Lan caught them in his room playing with the private stuff under his bed. And it suddenly occurred to Lan that the phone call might be to Grace, back in Adelaide. It had been less than a day, but if you were in love it probably would seem a long time apart, so of course he'd call and tell her about the trip (that was the water under the bridge part; they'd crossed the mighty Murray) and the carnival tomorrow and how they had to be there early.

He felt sorry now that he'd interrupted the call, and he made to go. But Spinner muttered a goodbye into the phone and hung up. He put the letter back in his pocket and said in his normal voice, 'What's up, matey? Shouldn't you be gettin' some shut-eye?'

Lan told him his concerns about waking up in time and Spinner said not to worry, Mr Warton would do enough of that, and he'd probably run around the corridors striking a breakfast gong. They both grinned.

'Sorry I interrupted your call, Spinner,' Lan said, and then added slyly, 'Were you speaking to someone special?'

'Special?'

'I thought maybe you were talking to a girlfriend.'

Spinner looked taken aback. 'Blimey, little pitchers have long ears. What made you think that?'

'Your voice sounded different.'

'Talk about Sherlock bloody Holmes. You'll be checkin' me room for cigarette butts next.'

'Why?' asked Lan, puzzled.

'Forget it.' Spinner cleared his throat. 'I was talkin' low so as not to wake up anyone.'

'Right.'

'Anyway, old geezers like me don't have girlfriends.' Lan was all set to tell him about Michael Douglas when Spinner added, 'They have lady friends.'

Lan grinned. 'Anyone I know?'

Spinner cuffed him. 'Get off to bed.'

Lan went off happily. He thought of waking Izram and telling him the Spinner and Grace romance was well on track but decided it could wait until morning.

Eight

Mr Warton, or somebody else — Lan was too sleepy to tell — did indeed rouse them with a loud knocking on the door at 7.15 and a flick-back of the curtains. By the time Lan fully awoke and sat up, Sam was sitting on his bed, fully dressed in his cricket clothes.

'Jeez, is it that late!' Lan scrambled out of bed in a panic.

'No, it's only 7.20. I woke up early, that's all.'

'Oh.' Lan saw now that Izram and Tomas were still in bed. 'I'll grab the first shower then.

Make those two get up, will you? We don't want to be late on the first day. What's the weather like?'

'Looks fine. It's not raining, anyway.'

Lan heard the other two come into the bathroom while he was in the shower, so he cut it short. He stepped out of the cubicle and began to dry himself.

'Why's he in his cricket gear?' Izram asked, jerking his head towards the bedroom.

'He got up early.'

'Didn't that master say last night there were changing rooms at this Bulleen place?'

Lan shrugged. 'Does it matter?'

'Well, I'm wearing shorts.'

'You can wear a skirt for all I care, fishwit.' Lan flicked him with his wet towel and Izram called him a vegiehead and flicked him back, and some of the good humour of their normal relationship was restored.

Sam called out that he was going downstairs. About five minutes later, as they were dressing, they heard a resounding boom echo through the corridors. 'That means brekkie,' Lan said. So Mr Warton really did hit a gong. He was glad they hadn't been woken by one, but it was a dramatic way of being summoned to breakfast. Like being in a temple or a palace.

The dining hall, when they entered, looked

very different from the previous evening. The curtains were pulled back and sunshine flooded in through large windows. A buffet had been set up at the servery where a queue had already formed, kept in motion by an anxious Mr Warton. The tables were now occupied by boys of all shapes, sizes and colours. Lan felt struck by a sudden shyness and perhaps everyone else felt the same because, despite the numbers, there was only a muted hum of voices. Then he spotted Spinner and Andy and some of the others sitting at the table they'd occupied last night, and they went and joined them.

Spinner was slurping tea and had a plate of fried eggs and rice in front of him. 'There's a regular United Nations buffet over there. Go and get some grub.'

They went over and Lan got in line behind Sam. 'We're queuing in Queue,' Lan said. Izram looked at him, perplexed, but Sam grinned and said, 'People who live in Kew must be Kewers.' They both laughed.

'That's a truly pathetic joke,' Izram said. 'Why isn't there any ordinary food?'

They looked at the warming dishes set out on the buffet table. As they had at dinner, St Paul's had made a commendable effort to be multicultural. There were dishes of eggs, boiled and fried, sliced meats and cheeses, congee, noodle soup and rice.

There were flat breads and chapattis, and fresh fruit.

Mr Warton, noticing their hesitation, hurried up. 'Everything all right? Orange juice and milk over there. Did anyone want tea? Jasmine? Green tea?'

'Hey brudda, why there no blackfella food?'

The loud voice rang out behind Lan. He turned, as did everyone else in the line. The speaker was a tall, lanky Aboriginal boy dressed in khaki shorts and a faded blue T-shirt, his unruly hair still damp from the shower. He stared accusingly at the housemaster.

'Well, umm …'

'Plenty noodles and rice. Plenty nip food. No bush tucker. That's discrimination, man.'

The whole dining hall fell silent. Mr Warton looked distressed. 'I'm sorry, nobody told me. Tell me what you want and I'll do my best to get it.'

'Too right. Here's what we want: baked beans, snags, white bread, Coco Pops, OK?'

Mr Warton looked relieved. 'I think we can get that.'

The boy grinned. 'You should see your face, man. You thinking snake and witchetty grubs, emu eggs, how I going to get blackfella food, right?'

The housemaster smiled weakly. 'Something like that.'

The boy laughed uproariously, but not unkindly, and ripples of laughter spread throughout the room. Lan thought it had been a pretty good joke. Mr Warton went into the kitchen and came back with boxes of cereal and loaves of white bread. 'Snags and baked beans tomorrow,' he promised.

'Good,' said Izram approvingly. 'And some Vegemite, please.'

'He really got old Worry-Wart, didn't he?' Andy said, when they carried their plates back to the table. 'Wonder which team he's with?'

'They're from the Alice,' Spinner said. 'Pretty good team, I hear. Called the Dead Reds.'

They looked at him in surprise. 'How'd you know that?' Andy asked.

'Met their coach last night. That's him over there. Says he comes from warrior stock. Better watch out.' Spinner caught the eye of a tall, solidly-built young man with close-cropped hair, and lifted his tea cup in greeting.

'Why are they called the Dead Reds?' Lan asked.

'Because they come from round Alice Springs. The Dead Centre, the Red Centre.'

'Well, it's better than being called the Alices,' Izram said, and they laughed. Lan noticed that Sam didn't even crack a grin, but looked across the table at Izram through narrowed eyes. He sighed inwardly. Were those two heading towards full-on aggro?

'And those really black kids are from the Tiwi Islands,' Spinner said, using a piece of chapatti to shovel up a mouthful of runny egg. Lan hoped Grace had never seen him eat breakfast.

'Where are the Tiwi Islands?' he asked.

'North of Darwin.'

'Are you allowed to say black?' Phon whispered.

'What else am I gunna say? Yellow with green spots?'

'*He* said blackfella,' Andy pointed out.

'That's like us calling ourselves nips,' said Lan.

'*You're* black,' Akram said, pointing to Satria.

'Am not! Not as black as him anyway.' Satria pointed to Tomas.

Tomas looked at his arm. 'Brown, not black.'

'You're all brown and yeller like a lot of cattle dogs and about as yippy,' said Spinner. 'All you need to worry about is how they play cricket.'

Lan, who up to that point had not been worried at all, suddenly felt a spurt of nervous adrenaline and looked around him with new eyes. These were his competitors for the Cup. Or some of them: Laura had mentioned local teams would also be competing. They couldn't all be Aboriginal: some of the boys at a table by the window had blond hair and fair skin. Yet they were clearly not Asian-Australians either. He pointed them out to Izram.

'Perhaps they're Dutch,' Izram said.

'*Dutch?*'

'Or from Germany or Switzerland or some other country that doesn't play cricket. We've got Sal in our team, haven't we?'

Lan sometimes forgot that Sal Catano was Italian-Australian, and therefore classified as a wog rather than a nip. But he had olive skin and dark hair and eyes and from the back you couldn't tell the difference. The boys over by the window were the only blue-eyed blonds in the dining hall and Lan was curious to find out who they were. He also wanted to meet the Aboriginal boy who had joked about bush tucker. He thought he knew what that was all about. Just because his own background was Vietnamese didn't mean he had to (or wanted to) eat noodle soup for breakfast.

His chance came when they were boarding the bus. An aisle seat was free next to the Aboriginal boy and on an impulse Lan paused and said, 'Can I sit here?'

'Nobody stoppin' ya.' He shifted slightly to make room.

'That was a pretty good joke of yours at breakfast,' Lan said.

The boy grinned. His teeth, large, white and even, looked capable of biting through a cricket ball. 'I shoulda asked for a croc steak, eh?'

'He probably would've tried to get you one.'

'Ah, he's OK. It's just that everybody down

south thinks of Aboriginals as singin' and dancin' or huntin' and fishin'. All the tourist stuff, you know. But in Alice lots of blackfellas have jobs. One of me uncles works at Imparja Television.'

'What's that?'

'An Aboriginal TV station, the only one in the whole country. I'm thinkin' of working there one day.'

'On TV?'

He laughed. 'Nah. I'm not good-lookin' enough. As a cameraman. I reckon that'd be an ace job. What d'you wanna do?'

Lan considered not telling him in case he sounded big-headed. Or in case he walked out onto the Bulleen playing field this morning and was bowled out first ball. But he couldn't immediately think of anything he wanted as much so he said simply, 'Play cricket for Australia.'

'Yeah?' His seatmate looked at him. 'You pretty good, are ya?'

'Not as good as I want to be. I haven't played that long.'

'Me neither. Not many blackfellas play cricket. Footy's more our game. I got four brothers and they all play footy. Aussie Rules, ya know, that's the number one sport. You c'n go anywhere to catch a game and usually one of your mob'll be playin'.'

A mob of what? Lan wondered, but didn't like to ask. Instead he said, 'How did you start?'

'Some fellas come up from Melbourne and held these coachin' clinics and gave us free bats and T-shirts and all the gear, then after they went away we got this team together called the Dead Reds, and a coach — that's him over there, the big bloke — and sponsors and started playin'.' He gestured around the bus. 'Most these teams started like that. Some of 'em are real bush rats. Don't reckon they'd even seen a wicket before.'

Lan told him about the Nips. His seatmate seemed impressed. 'That's pretty wicked, doin' it all yourselves like that. Reckon you c'n beat us?'

'We might,' Lan said cautiously.

'You'll be lucky. So, what's ya name, man? Jes' so I'll know when ya start playin' for Australia.'

'Lan Nguyen.'

'Jermaine Miller. And I got news for you, Lan-man. You might play for Australia one day but the Dead Reds are gunna win this Cup!' He half-rose in his seat and yelled the final words, which were answered by a resounding cheer from his team-mates.

'Dead Heads, more like,' called Andy.

'There must be a tap around here somewhere, I can hear a drip,' Jermaine said loudly.

'Up the Nips! *Woah oh, the nips are getting bigger!*' sang Andy. The other Nips took up the chorus, raising their voices as various other loyal yells echoed around the bus.

'That's our team song,' explained Lan, a little worried that the Harmony Cup carnival wasn't getting off to a very friendly start. 'Have you got one?'

'We got a war cry!' Jermaine said, baring his teeth.

They were spared the performance of this as just then Laura took the microphone and announced they were at Bulleen. The bus turned off the road and headed for a pavilion and clubrooms set in the surrounds of green playing fields. The car park was full and there were kids in white everywhere.

Team Meeting — The Captain's Notes

Harmony Cup, Friday, Day One

- Well done everybody: your commitment and attitude have been great (even if so far Onya is only one to write a poem).
- Welcome to Sam: his first match with Nips.
- Our training has been v. good, thanks to Spinner. This is the start of big things for team.
- Remember our Multicultural Day match ?

  We wanted to win.
  We did it for each other.
  We worked hard and had terrific team spirit.
  We played the game and played fairly.

This time we don't know what the opposition is like. So I can only say:

Batsmen: stay focused.

Bowlers: take early wickets (take late wickets also)

Everyone: don't forget: it's normal to be nervous (so are they)

• Dig deep and believe you can achieve anything. Good luck!

We arrived on the train
In lots of rain,
But then it got sunny,
Melbourne weather is funny.
We will win the cricket
If we don't lose our wicket.

Tomas Nuñez

Nine

The Nips had drawn the team from the Tiwi Islands, who were called the Hunters. They wore shorts and yellow T-shirts which hung to their knees. Lan talked briefly to the captain, Russell, who told him they were called Hunters because that's what they were. 'Tiwi people like hunting and going off for a bush holiday. We get wallaby, or go fishing, get mangrove worms, crabs, plenty of good tucker about.'

'No shops or takeaway?' Lan asked. He couldn't imagine having to hunt for the food on your table. Worms didn't appeal much either.

Russell patted his stomach and grinned. 'Oh yeah. Lot of takeaway junk too.'

The Hunters won the toss and elected to bat. Lan was downcast: it seemed a bad omen. The first duty of the captain was to win the toss. 'Win the toss and win the match,' that's what they said.

'Don't let it worry ya,' Spinner said, noticing his expression. 'Steve Waugh's lost countless tosses and it hasn't done the team any harm, has it?'

That was true. And at least now he didn't have to decide whether to bat or bowl. One would be the wrong decision. Then you felt responsible if the team lost, even though it was very easy to say, 'Well, of course we should have batted first,' *after* the match. Anyway, it probably didn't matter much in these first sixteen-over matches.

'What's your plan?' Lan asked Andy as he marked out his run-up for the first over.

'To land the ball on the pitch.'

'That's all?'

'The only plan I ever have,' Andy said, 'is hoping I won't stuff up. Works for me.'

How could you argue with that? Lan set the field. The Hunters' opening batsman stood at the wicket with a grin on his face nearly as wide as his legs.

Andy took a long run-up. With his first ball he bowled the opening batsman, whose grin quickly vanished. He trudged off, dejected. Lan wanted to tell him his technique was all wrong, but decided it probably wasn't the right time.

Russell, the captain, was the next to go. Lan avoided his gaze as he, too, trudged off. The third batsman came in, looking terrified, and barely lifted his bat. When he was bowled, a vast look of relief swept his face. He whipped off his gloves and scuttled off the pitch.

The batsmen were sharing pads and they couldn't change them quickly enough. Almost as soon as they got their pads on they had to take them off again. Andy took five wickets in his first two overs.

Lan, at first exhilarated, also felt a little embarrassed. And yes, sorry. You were allowed to feel sorry for the opposition, weren't you? He remembered how inadequate he'd felt as a raw recruit that first day at the North Illaba Cricket Club.

Andy came off on a high. 'Jeez, how easy is this game?'

'I thought you didn't have a plan,' Lan said.

'I didn't. I just kept running in and bowling full tosses and yorkers and they kept missing them. You can go in now and clean them up.'

It was the obvious thing to do. It was the professional thing to do. Instead, Lan sent Tomas in, much to Tomas's surprise.

'You sure?' he asked. 'I not bowl like you and Andy, no way.'

Lan knew that, but it was why he was sending Tomas in. Andy had scared the pants off the opposition. Normally, that would be cause for celebration. But *this* team …

From behind the wicket Izram caught his eye and his expression was plain. *What are you doing? Not Onya, not now.*

Lan found it hard to articulate, even to himself, why he'd backed off. It had something to do with Russell's friendliness and the little black stick legs of the opening batsman and the fear on the face of the third. Sending Tomas in would give him confidence and them breathing space and let them chalk up a few runs. The Nips were going to win anyhow, but it didn't have to be a complete slaughter.

'Did I do the right thing?' Lan asked Spinner after the match.

'We won, didn't we?'

'Is that an answer?'

'The best.'

'So it wouldn't have been right if we hadn't won?'

Spinner chuckled. 'Lose and everyone's an

expert. All the world and his dog will tell ya what you did wrong.'

'Some of the others think I was a bit soft. I mean, bringing in Onya.'

'And moving young Phon and Satto up the batting order?'

'Yeah, that too. I wanted to give them a bit of confidence.'

'Matey, we're not playin' Test cricket. You made those decisions because you knew you were gunna win anyway, so it's all right with me.'

Lan was satisfied. They loaded their plates from the lunch buffet and sat down at one of the tables on the veranda of the pavilion, the other Nips straggling up to join them. The day had got steadily warmer and Lan wished he was wearing shorts instead of his long cricket pants.

They were halfway through their sandwiches when a young man wearing dark glasses strolled up. The sleeves of his crisp blue shirt were rolled to the elbows and an identity card was clipped to his pocket. 'So, how's it going? Everything on track?' he asked cheerfully. They all said that it was.

'Are you a Hospitality Attendant?' Lan asked. He was going to tell him that the hospitality had so far been excellent.

The man laughed heartily. He said, 'No, I'm a media liaison officer.' He introduced himself to

Spinner, and shook hands. 'You've got a quality team there,' he said.

Lan hoped that was complimentary. He'd only ever heard the word applied to fruit. 'Oranges very good,' his father would say. 'Best quality.' Or, 'Low price for cabbage this week, all poor quality.' So what did 'quality' on its own mean?

The two men chatted about the morning's play. 'It's all about momentum, of course,' the younger man said.

'Is that right?' said Spinner.

'I think all sport is about building momentum.'

'Then we've started the momentum running in our favour by winning the first match,' Spinner said. He winked at Lan. 'Nice to have a win under our belts.'

The man wished them further luck and went off to chat at other tables.

'What's he mean, building momentum?' Izram asked, through a mouthful of roast beef baguette.

'Blowed if I know,' Spinner said. 'Bit of a swankpot, I reckon. Media liaison officer!' He sniffed. 'When I played, we had a coach and a part-time manager. That was it. Now the team's got a psychologist, a nutritionist, a fitness trainer, a physio, a coach, a dietitian, a fulltime manager, a media liaison officer and God knows who else.'

'And a feng shui master,' said Andy, straight-faced.

'What?'

'Feng shui. It's Chinese. It gets your stuck energies moving.'

Spinner snorted. 'A session in the nets will get your energies movin', not some mumbo-jumbo twaddle. Players today don't do enough net practice.'

Izram rolled his eyes at Lan in a way that said clearly, *The old boy's off on one of his 'We-never-had-it-so-soft-players-today-don't-know-they're-born' rants.* Lan knew that Spinner and Mr Hussein could carry on happily in this vein for hours, assuring each other that the modern game of cricket had sunk to appalling levels of (and this depended on their mood) wimpishness or anarchy. In an effort to change the subject, he said quickly, 'Spinner, why do we put it under our belts?'

'Put what?'

'A win. You might put a win in your pocket, I could understand that, but how do you put one under your belt? Why do they say that? Cricketers don't even wear belts. Neither do footballers.'

'Or soccer players,' said Sal.

'Or swimmers, or basketball players,' added Akram.

'Orright, orright, point made. I dunno why or

how you put a win under your belt, let's just get another one,' Spinner said.

Laura Jolly came up. 'A big win this morning, Nips, well done!' She sat down so that Spinner, who had risen from his seat at her approach, would also sit down.

'The Hunters tried really hard,' Lan said, 'but I don't think they've had our experience.'

Laura smiled. 'They're coming along. We went to the Tiwis last year with Karen Rolton and Jason Gillespie and conducted some coaching clinics. The kids were really enthusiastic. They love getting out of the classroom to muck around with a bat and ball. You have to make it fun. Not too much hard work or they drop out. But be warned: we're pairing you with a bit of stronger competition this afternoon.'

She took Spinner off to introduce him to some of the other coaches and adults.

'Whose Karen Rolton?' Lan asked. Izram, usually their best source of cricket information, shrugged. The others looked equally blank.

Then Sam spoke up. 'She's vice-captain of the Australian women's cricket team.' They all looked at him. 'She's from Adelaide, actually.'

'Oh,' said Andy dismissively. 'Women's cricket.'

'She's a terrific player,' Sam said.

'Maybe. But …'

'But what?' Sam demanded. He looked around the table.

'It's not the same, is it?' Izram said. 'The game's not as hard as the men's.'

'For your information,' Sam said, 'Rolton's highest Test score's 209 not out, including twenty-nine fours and a six.'

Izram made a face of grudging acknowledgement. 'So she's the Steve Waugh of women's cricket.'

'Maybe he's the Karen Rolton of men's cricket,' Sam retorted, an edge in his voice.

'Oh, c'mon!'

'Well, try this then. Belinda Clark, the captain, holds the record for the highest ever One Day International score by a male *or* female: 229 not out.'

Lan gaped, as did several of the others. Sam didn't let up. 'In her first Test she opened the batting and made a century. She scored the first double century — male *or* female — in ODIs. She's scored most runs for Australia. *And* her team won the World Cup three times in succession. Good enough for you?'

Lan was doubly impressed. First, by the statistics (who knew a woman could play like that!) and second, by the fact that Sam knew all the statistics. But Izram wasn't quite ready to concede defeat. 'OK, but how would she go against a Warnie or a Tendulkar, hey?'

'Don't know about that,' said Spinner, seemingly appearing from nowhere, 'but in 1994 at the Sydney Cricket Ground, Zoe Goss, only woman on the team, dismissed the Windies' star batsman, Brian Lara. Caused a sensation.' Izram opened his mouth, prepared to argue. 'As for good battin',' Spinner went on, anticipating him, 'that's not about physical strength. No reason why a girl can't be a champion.'

Izram shut his mouth, conceding defeat, but looking uncharacteristically sulky. Sam said nothing but couldn't quite hide the triumph in his eyes. What was going on between those two? Lan worried. He liked them both, but not when they were together. Whatever the source of the conflict, it couldn't be good for team spirit.

Captain's Diary Friday 19 January

All the wickets we take, all the
 runs we score
Are never enough, we must want
 more,
If we do we will be the winner,
And a lot of it will be thanks to
 Spinner.

Sal Catano

It's always good to get an early one under our belts but the game with the Hunters did not really stretch us. Plus I was worried that we might have peaked early and from then on it would all be downhill. Thankfully, that didn't happen. And I thought Russell, the captain of the Hunters, would be upset and not want to talk to me but I saw him later and he was OK. He said, 'This is deadly, coming here and mixing with all you blokes and playing real cricket. I want to do something really deadly, not just hang around or be a truck driver or something.' So now he reckons he might be a cricketer.

The first thing that happened when we arrived at Bulleen this morning was a traditional welcome. An Aboriginal man said that we were on the land of the Wurundjeri people and as traditional owners they would like to welcome us. This included some didgeridoo-playing that was awesome. It sent a shiver down my back. After that there were speeches (some went on a bit too much about Living in Harmony, I thought) and then we all got bags from the Australian Cricket Board full of free stuff — stickers, swap cards, photos, a pen, cap, drinks bottle, sunblock and zinc cream, and tip sheets, like How to Bat Under Pressure (which should be very useful!).

After lunch, we played a local team called the Footscray Fighters. They were mostly nips but not as good as us. They won the toss (I lost again!) and elected to bat. That meant I was into it almost straight away. (I like a bit of batting first, it sort of gets me into the game.) My first few deliveries were pretty rough. I couldn't seem to control the ball at all. Then I got my first wicket in the first ball of my second over and it was probably the worst I bowled. It was short and really wide and when the batsman smashed it I thought, Good one, Lan, that's a four. But then Sam dived almost full length and caught it! I felt like kissing him! (I didn't.) Anyway, I took five wickets (the first five wicket haul in my career!), and we bowled them out for seventy-nine and won by eighty-two runs.

Sam was a star. He got his forty runs so easily — five were boundaries, and one sixer. Everybody applauded, even the people standing around watching the games. I asked him whether he wanted to bowl and he did, and took one wicket. It would have been two, but Iz missed what looked like a pretty easy catch behind the stumps, which is not like him. We all groaned and Sam had a look on his face like he thought it was deliberate. Would Iz do something like that? I don't think so, but there's something going on between those two. Any division in the team could affect our chances so this is something I'll have to deal with (but I'm not sure how).

I found out that Jermaine is captain of the Dead Reds. They won both their matches today, too. Spinner walked around and looked at the other games and he said they are the ones to beat, although a team called the Tasmanian Tigers looked good. The blond boys I saw in the dining room are in this team. Spinner says they are Aborigines, everyone in the team is Aboriginal. I was pretty surprised. So much for them being Dutch!

The Melbourne teams shout a lot. I guess it's their way of revving up. Spinner says it comes from footy. The Footscray Fighters were really pumped up to win. When the game began they all yelled, 'Big start, Fighters! Big start!' and the slips kept calling out things like, 'C'mon, Huy! Nice and tight!' Andy said that one of the slips who is Chinese sledged him when he was walking to the crease. I said, 'If you answer back he knows he's getting to you and he'll only do it more. Let your bat do the talking.' Andy said, 'Yeah, I tried that, but my bat doesn't speak Cantonese, so I gave him a mouthful.' This is not exactly in the spirit of the Harmony Cup.

We have now been away from home for thirty-six hours and twenty minutes but already there have been some quarrels and complaints. Iz said that Onya talks in his sleep in a foreign language — Spanish or whatever they speak in El Salvador. I said, 'Well, you can't expect him to talk in English, he hardly knows any.' Iz said he didn't want him to talk in any language, he just wanted him to shut up. I joked and said maybe Onya was composing his poem, but Iz didn't laugh. Then Sal complained that Hiroki grinds his teeth and Jemal complained that Phon got up 'hundreds of times' through the night to go to the toilet. Spinner said to give them all ear plugs.

It's a difficult job, being a touring captain. At home, everyone disappears after play or practice and you don't see each other again for a while. But here, we are eating and sleeping and playing and travelling together every day. So while I think Living in Harmony is a nice idea, I also think it can be hard when you try to do it.

At the end of the afternoon they posted up the results in the pavilion, along with tomorrow's draws. It was heaps complicated with all the different points. But the Nips are looking good. Our match tomorrow is against a local team called the Dragons. And then we got some really good news: we were off to the MCG!

Ten

From the gloom of the underpass they walked out into the late afternoon sunshine. Lan stopped dead and his mouth fell open. He swivelled, slowly. 'Wow!' he breathed, and it seemed a weak response. No picture he'd seen had adequately conveyed the stupendous dimensions of the MCG or how insignificant you might feel in the middle of its impressive arena. It wasn't an oval at all; nothing remotely resembling Adelaide's red-brick picket-fence charm. This was a stadium, a colosseum, a place where gladiators might fight to the death.

'Six lighting towers each eighty metres high

and weighing 130 tonnes ... a total of 840 globes, each 2000 watts, each focused on a particular part of the pitch ...' The guide in the navy-striped blazer dutifully trotted out the statistics, none of which meant much to Lan. He focused instead on the Great Southern Stand directly in front of him, its rows of empty metal-grey seats shining like rivers of silver, and populated it with cheering crowds applauding his heroic Test innings.

'Follow me, please,' said the guide. 'I'm now going to take you onto the *hallowed turf* itself.'

'Howzat!' cried Izram, looking at his watch and digging his elbow into Lan's side. 'I win! You owe me a dollar.' The two of them had placed a bet on how soon the magic phrase would be uttered. Within four and a half minutes of the start of the tour, Izram had guessed, and he had underestimated by only forty-three seconds.

They followed the guide through the gate and onto the grass. 'Take a photo of me with my bat,' Lan said. He'd brought it along just in case he spotted a famous face; you never knew your luck in a place like this. He held it out in front of him, not quite posing, feeling a little self-conscious.

Izram snapped off a picture and Lan tried to imagine what it must be like to take a wicket or hit a sixer in this mighty arena and to have eighty thousand cricket enthusiasts applauding and cheering you. On the other hand … He glanced up at the giant electronic scoreboard-cum-television-screen and tried to imagine what it would be like to fail in front of eighty thousand people. You'd have to make the long walk back to the players' gate while the instant replays ran. You could watch yourself get out six times.

'Did you ever take a wicket here, Spinner?' he asked, rejoining the group.

'A few,' Spinner said.

The guide's ears pricked up. 'You've played cricket here, sir?'

'It was a long time ago. I'd need a map to find the wicket now.'

Lan said proudly, 'He played Test cricket. He was famous. They called him the Mystery Spinner.'

The guide looked astonished. 'Good Lord! Then you must have been Clarrie McGinty?'

'Still am,' Spinner said. 'Or I was last time I looked.'

'Of course. Excuse me. It's the surprise. Well, good heavens! What a turn-up for the books! I'm proud to shake your hand, Mr McGinty.' He held out his hand and a pink-faced Spinner shook it. But Lan could tell he was pleased by the recognition.

'Our museum curator will be thrilled to meet you,' said the guide.

Spinner looked rather less pleased. 'Probably

wants to stuff me and put me in a glass case, along with the other old relics,' he muttered to Lan as they left the arena and climbed the steps to the players' rooms.

Lan thought the whole MCG was a bit like a museum. The interiors, anyway, which were dim and gloomy, with dark timber panelling, corridors lined with framed black and white photographs of ancient, bewhiskered cricketers, and endless glass-fronted cabinets containing historic bats, balls and stumps. He wondered if there was a similar museum at Wimbledon full of old racquets and ancient tennis nets.

Sam had stopped to look at the photographs. 'He looks like a walrus,' Lan joked, pointing to one stout player with a long drooping moustache.

'I haven't seen any woman cricketers, have you?' Sam murmured. 'Not one in all these displays.'

Izram overheard the comment. 'Well, that oughta tell you something,' he said.

'It does,' Sam said emphatically.

'Not that again,' Lan said, frowning at Izram.

'He's the one who keeps banging on about women's cricket. Why are you so interested, anyway?' Izram demanded of Sam.

'My sister plays, all right? And everybody ought to be interested. The men's team aren't the only world champions.'

'So you keep telling us.'

'Seems some people have cloth ears.'

'And some people have one-track minds.'

'Hey, cool it,' Lan said.

'Hurry along, please!' called the guide from further up the corridor. Then he remembered his famous guest. 'Are we going too fast for you, sir?'

'No, you're not,' snapped Spinner. 'I jes' stopped to look at the 1891 Test teams.' He looked around and beckoned to Lan and Izram. 'There he is, that's the great Dr W.G. Grace.' He jabbed his finger at a giant of man with a belligerent expression in his eyes and a great dark bush of a beard obscuring his lower face.

'He is so fat!' exclaimed Izram.

Lan, too, was surprised. So this was the famous cricketer who had given Grace her nickname. She could hardly be flattered.

'Ah, they were all big blokes in them days,' Spinner said.

'Probably 'cos they didn't have dietitians and nutritionists and trainers,' Izram said slyly.

Spinner pretended not to hear.

'You should buy a postcard of him and send it to Grace,' Lan suggested, thinking it might help keep their romance bubbling.

'Nah,' Spinner said.

They caught up with the others and tracked

through the players' dining room and into the changing room, both of them soulless and utilitarian. Lan didn't quite know what he'd been expecting, but surely for the finest players in the nation the MCG could do better than old laminated tables and a pie warmer, and this dingy room lined with scuffed steel lockers and smelling of old socks and liniment? Butler service, red carpet and crystal chandeliers wouldn't be too much. At the very least, a squirt of air freshener.

'Things haven't changed much,' Spinner said.

'Ah, but they will,' the guide assured him. He launched into details of the planned $400 million redevelopment of the ground.

Izram was circumnavigating the room, seemingly fascinated by the lockers. He opened and closed each one, as if unwilling to believe they could all be exactly the same. 'Hoping to find a baggy green left behind?' joked Lan.

'Listen to this,' called out Hiroki, and read from a notice on the wall. '*What to do in case of pitch invasion or bomb threat.*'

'Run like hell?' suggested Andy.

'All right lads, follow me!' called the guide, and was on the trot again. For an old guy, thought Lan, he was pretty quick on his feet.

Upstairs, it was a lot ritzier. In the Long Room, where members came to drink and dine, there were thick crimson monogrammed carpets, ornate plasterwork and enough chandeliers to light up Flinders Street. 'Men only in here,' said Spinner approvingly, looking around at the bar and the long blue leather couches in front of the large windows which looked straight down on the wickets.

'Not any more, Mr McGinty,' the guide corrected. 'Ladies have been admitted since 1984.'

'Get away!' exclaimed Spinner, looking stunned.

'I thought you believed in equality in sport?' Sam said.

'In sport, yeah. But not in *here*. Some things are sacred.'

Lan peered at more cricket bats in more glass cases, and tried to make out who the autographs belonged to. Izram was more interested in details of the luncheon menu, as posted on a display menu at the entrance to the dining room. 'Check out today's special,' he said, reading. '*Soup and Roast of the Day, $27*. You can get a whole Banquet Supreme for less than that at the Bukhara.' He took one of the restaurant cards out of his pocket and slipped it into a corner of the menu board.

'You can't do that!' exclaimed Lan, glancing around him worriedly.

'Why can't I?'

''Cos it's not a public notice board, that's why.

And for another thing, this is Melbourne, so what's the point? The Bukhara's about 700 ks west.'

'People travel, don't they? And if the food at Adelaide Oval's as boring as this, they might be glad to know where to get a good curry. I stuck cards in all the lockers, too. You never know, Steve Waugh or Adam Gilchrist might turn up one night.'

So that was what he'd been up to in the changing room! 'You're a good salesman,' Lan conceded, and Izram nodded happily. He snapped off a photo of the menu board to show his father.

'Something to interest you here!' called the guide, already out of the Long Room and halfway down the stairs.

'I don't think so,' Andy muttered. 'Not unless it's a double cheeseburger and fries.'

'I'm starving,' Akka said.

'Is very long tour,' said Tomas.

The sense of history was beginning to get a bit oppressive, Lan thought. He wondered if they'd ever get to see a live cricketer. The guide, his face alight with anticipation, was standing in front of yet another framed photograph. 'You'll know this team, Mr McGinty!'

Spinner put on his glasses and peered at it. He started ticking off the names, then abruptly stopped. 'Too depressin'. Most of 'em are dead.'

'Not that one,' said the guide, pointing.

'That's a bloke called McGinty. I wish to God I looked like that now.'

In the photo, as in the one that hung in the Chappell Bar at the Adelaide Oval, the young Clarence McGinty was smiling and handsome, his dark hair gleaming, his frame loose and athletic. Lan was moved by the tone of regret in the old man's voice and he said, 'When people think of you, that's how they'll remember you, Spinner.'

'Until they clap eyes on me,' he grumbled.

Why was Spinner concerned about his appearance, Lan wondered? He never had been before. Lan wanted to assure him that it didn't matter in the least. All old people looked more or less alike anyway. He couldn't tell whether someone was forty-five or sixty-five, and he was sure none of the other Nips could either.

'And finally, the museum and library,' said the guide, beaming as if he'd left the best for last and seemingly oblivious to the lack of enthusiasm on the faces of his group. 'Follow me! … along here … this way!'

Lan stopped dead. They were heading away from the arena and he'd completely forgotten to get his piece of hallowed turf. He caught Izram's arm. 'Let me have one of your empty film canisters, willya?'

'What for?'

'Tell you later. If anyone notices, say I've gone to the toilet. Won't be a sec.'

Being somewhat disoriented by their rambling tour, it took him much longer than that to even find his way back to the pitch. When he did, he wasn't quite brazen enough to stride out to the middle. Instead, he contented himself with bending down just inside the boundary fence and scooping out a small square of turf with the aid of a twenty cent coin. He was just poking it into the film canister when he heard a stern voice say, 'And what d'you think you're doing, kid?'

Lan nearly dropped the canister. His mouth went dry. He turned, his face diffused with guilt.

A man was standing on the bottom of the steps that led to the players' rooms. Where had he come from? And who was he? He wasn't wearing the blazer that all the tour guides wore but he looked and spoke authoritatively. His eyes were hidden by dark glasses but the rest of his face didn't seem very pleased.

Lan gulped. What was the penalty for digging up the hallowed turf of the mighty G? Three years in gaol, probably. He held out the canister. 'It's a souvenir.'

'What if everyone dug up a piece of the pitch?'

That's what grown-ups always said, Lan thought: *What if everyone did that?* If everyone did it,

OK, you'd certainly have a problem. But he was only one person. And where were the signs saying 'Do Not Dig'?

He decided this was unlikely to be an effective defence. He said nothing.

'What are you doing here, anyway?' the man demanded.

'I'm with a tour group. They're up there.' Lan waved vaguely towards the stands. 'My team's playing in a cricket carnival this weekend. We're from Adelaide.' *See, I'm not a Victorian, I'm not a Melbournite, I'm foreign, I didn't know.*

'Do you always carry your bat with you everywhere?'

Lan stooped to pick it up. 'I thought I'd get an autograph if I met someone famous.'

'And have you?'

'Not yet. There's lots of famous cricketers here but they're all dead.'

The man's lips twitched. He held out his hand. 'I might as well sign it then.'

Lan didn't want to give it to him — he didn't want some unknown's autograph on his bat, even if he was an MCG official — but he didn't like to say no. It would sound rude and besides, he'd been caught out doing something that was apparently highly illegal; it would be more diplomatic to hand it over. He did.

'Got a pen?'

Lan handed that over too. The man took it and signed his name on the bat.

'Thanks,' Lan said, barely glancing at it. 'Well, I better go. The tour's probably over.'

'Sorry about all those dead cricketers.'

'That's OK.'

'Good luck in the carnival. Hope you win.'

'Thanks. Seeya.' He was nice after all, Lan thought.

By the time he caught up with it again, the tour group was winding its way back to the entrance foyer. Izram was dawdling in the rear, obviously looking out for him. 'Where've you been?' he demanded.

'I went to get some turf. Nearly got nicked, too. Here, have a look.'

But Izram wasn't interested in bits of dirt, however hallowed. 'Listen, something's happened. About Sam.'

Lan sighed. He was sick of Izram and Sam and their petty snipings. 'Iz, I don't really care.'

'While you were away, guess what I saw him do?'

'Iz, leave the guy alone. You seem to have Sam on the brain or something. What's the matter with you?'

'It's not me, it's him.'

'It's you! You're always having a go at him. It's bad for the team and it's affecting your game. Look at that missed catch today.'

Izram stared at him. 'You think I did that on purpose?'

'I didn't say that.'

'That's what you meant.' Izram looked outraged. 'You think I'm not pulling my weight as wicket-keeper! You think I'm sabotaging the team.'

'No, I don't. Stop telling me what I think.'

'If there's a saboteur in the team it's definitely not me.'

Lan turned away. 'Drop it, Iz. I don't want to hear any more, OK?'

Andy and Akram came up. 'There's a shop in the foyer that sells MCG stuff,' Andy said. 'We were thinking: what about having a whip round and buying Spinner a present? You know, as a thank-you for coming with us and helping us?'

Lan looked at Andy in surprise. 'This was your idea?'

'Yeah. Why?'

'Nothing. It's a good idea.' Lan was only surprised that Andy had come up with it. 'What do you reckon? A tie or a pair of socks?' Akram asked. 'The shirts are heaps expensive.'

Lan had only ever seen Spinner wear a tie once, and that had been last year, at the Supporters'

Dinner. Like all of Spinner's clothes, it had seen better days. The old man could do with a smart new tie. On the other hand, he sometimes wore odd socks. But a tie would be more visible. 'A tie,' he said.

'Yeah, that's what we thought, too.'

Andy had noticed his bat. 'Hey, you got an autograph!' He grabbed it. 'Who'd you meet, you lucky dude? I haven't seen anyone famous.'

'He's not famous. I don't know why I let him sign it. He was just some guy hanging around the stands. I might try to wash it off.'

Andy was peering at the autograph. 'I wouldn't,' he said. 'This says Ricky Ponting. Everyone says he'll be Test captain in a year or two.'

Eleven

The autograph and the details of its acquisition was the chief topic of conversation on the trip back to St Paul's. The signature was compared to the one on the Ricky Ponting swap card and pronounced genuine. Everybody thought it a huge joke that their cricket-obsessed captain had failed to recognise one of the star players. Lan's explanation that Ponting hadn't been wearing whites and that his eyes had been hidden by sunglasses cut no ice. 'Face it, Lanno,' Andy chortled. 'Unless he's in full cricket gear with his name on the back of his shirt, a ball in his right hand and a meat pie in his left, you'd walk straight past Shane Warne.'

'Yeah, right,' said Lan, grinning.

His film canister of hallowed turf had also excited interest. 'Wish I'd thought of that,' said Akram enviously, a desire that was echoed by so many in the bus that Lan began to see the point of Ponting's argument. 'I shouldn't have taken it, should I?' he asked Spinner.

'Too late now, matey.'

'He wouldn't report me, would he?'

'Ponting? Nah. He was probably havin' a lend of ya. How does he know who you are, anyway?'

'I told him I was from Adelaide, that we were playing in a carnival here.'

'Well, you're not likely to see him again, so I'd stop worryin'.'

Back at St Paul's, Mr Warton met them with the news that a barbecue had been arranged for the visiting teams and that they were welcome to use the school swimming pool. It had been a long hot day and the announcement was greeted with cheers.

'I didn't bring my bathers!' someone lamented. There were plenty of helpful suggestions.

'Go in the nuddy!'

'Wear yer underdaks!'

'Wear your box!'

'One worries about pool safety, of course,'

Mr Warton confided to Spinner. 'But they are quite mature boys, aren't they? And we do have you and the other adults on hand to supervise.'

'Not me,' said Spinner bluntly. 'Me swimmin' days, not to mention me swim-n-rescue days, are long over. Besides, I'm otherwise engaged this evenin'. You'd better sign up one of the young blokes.' He gestured towards the muscular coach of the TopEnders. 'There's yer man. Believe he wrestles crocs in his spare time.'

Mr Warton, a frown creasing his brow, trotted off. Lan, who had overheard the conversation, said, 'Does that mean you're going somewhere tonight, Spinner?'

'That's about it, matey.'

'You're not staying for the barbecue?' Lan's surprise was evident: it was not like Spinner to turn down the opportunity for a good feed.

'Made other arrangements. And I'm trustin' you to see everyone behaves themselves and gets to bed on time.'

Lan nodded. 'Sure. But where are you going?'

'I'm meetin' someone. Someone I haven't seen for a long time.'

'Someone you used to play with?'

'Someone I used to know when I was playin'.'

'What, like an umpire or a coach or something?'

'Blimey, what is this, an interrogation? Can't a bloke go out for a feed without facing a third degree?'

'I just wondered where you're going for dinner.'

'To a friend's place. If that's all right with you.'

'What if something happens and we need to get in touch?' Lan asked.

'Warton's here, ain't he?'

'We should still have a phone number,' Lan insisted. 'What if the barbecue burns down the school? What if someone drowns in the pool? What if —'

'Orright, orright, I'll leave you a number before I go.' Spinner stomped off.

What was he so touchy about? Lan wondered. Why hadn't he wanted to say where he was going and with whom? Was it possible he was going on a date? And if so, what did that say about his relationship with Grace?

He needed to talk to Izram about this, but since their altercation back at the MCG Izram had maintained an angry distance. He'd sat apart from him in the bus and, ignoring Lan, had raced off to the dorms with the others. Nevertheless, Lan went off to find him. He and Izram were the only ones who understood how important Spinner's romantic life was to the future of the team.

Upstairs, the corridors were empty and their room looked like a whirlwind had just blown in through the window with clothes, underwear, bags and gear strewn over the beds and floor. Sam, the only occupant, lay barefoot on his bed reading a magazine. He was dressed in jeans and T-shirt.

'Where's everybody?' Lan asked.

'Gone to the pool.'

'Aren't you going too?'

Sam flipped a page. 'Can't be bothered. I don't like swimming anyway.'

Lan stood, irresolute. He wanted to go to the pool and he needed to find Izram, but he didn't like the idea of leaving Sam up here, alone.

Sam looked up from *Inside Cricket*. 'What's the matter?'

'It's Spinner.'

'Is he ill?'

'No, it's not that.' How much could he, should he, tell Sam? He sat down on the edge of the bed. 'All of a sudden he's stressing about his age and how he's an old crock, specially compared to the other coaches. He got a bit depressed looking at those old photos at the G.'

'Yeah, I noticed.'

'He never used to be like that.'

Sam put down his magazine. 'It might be the coach thing. But if he's more worried about how he looks … He's not married, is he?' Lan shook his head. 'Maybe he's in love. And perhaps the person he's in love with thinks he's too old. That'd make you depressed, wouldn't it?'

Would it ever! Lan was thunderstruck. Why hadn't he thought of that? It was so obvious to him now: Grace must have rejected the old guy. Hadn't Izram said that they'd left the Bukhara separately after their dinner date? No wonder Spinner had refused to buy her a postcard of W.G. Grace. And now he was going off to meet someone else. A Melburnian!

He told Sam about the relationship, and how he and Izram were trying their best to promote it because Grace was a friend of the Nips and a big cricket fan. 'We don't want him to marry anyone who might stop him coaching us,' Lan explained.

'I bet that's it,' Sam said. 'The only time my sister stresses about the way she looks is when she's trying to hook a new boyfriend. Then she goes on a diet, has her hair done and buys new clothes. Especially new underwear.'

Lan thought it was probably a long time since Spinner had bought new underwear, judging by the shapeless grey garments he'd seen in his room last night. 'What can we do to help?' he asked. 'We can hardly take him shopping or to the hairdresser's.'

'Maybe you could drop a few hints.'

Lan frowned. 'How would I do that?'

'I don't know. Maybe point out to him old people who look groovy. You could just say something like, "Doesn't Paul McCartney look great? You'd never think he was sixty."'

'Is he?' said Lan, startled.

'I think so. Near enough, anyway. Mick Jagger's even older.'

Lan thought about this. 'Wouldn't that make him even more depressed because he didn't look as good as them?'

'It might inspire him. 'Specially if you make him think it's all to do with clothes and haircut.'

'It's worth a try, I guess.' Lan decided to speak to Izram about it. 'Thanks for your help.'

'You're welcome.'

Lan got up and rummaged in his bag for his bathers. 'Sure you won't come for a swim?' he asked, sitting on his own bed and ripping off his socks and sneakers.

Sam picked up his magazine and buried his face in it again. 'No thanks. I'll catch up with you at the barbecue.'

Pulling a clean T-shirt over his bathers and grabbing a towel, Lan slipped on a pair of thongs and went downstairs again. He exited through the back door, drawn by the tantalising smell of grilling meat and the yells coming from the fenced-off pool just beyond the lawns. He soon spotted Izram, who was horsing around with Andy and some of the others mid-pool. Lan called out to him, and jumped in.

The water felt wonderful, cold and refreshing. Lan surfaced, shaking the drops from his face. 'How's it going, Iz?'

Izram found himself in something of a dilemma. Lan had caught him having a good time, which meant he could hardly now revert to his pre-pool sulk. Once you had unsulked, you couldn't then re-sulk. On the other hand, he didn't want to let Lan off lightly: he hadn't shown his displeasure quite long enough. He compromised by avoiding eye contact and giving a non-committal grunt, which could mean anything.

'I have to talk to you about Spinner,' Lan said.

Izram grunted again.

Lan told him his theory — well, Sam's theory really, but he had enough sense not to mention that to Izram — about Spinner being blighted in love. 'He asked Grace to marry him, see, and Grace must have said no because she thought he was too old. So now he's going out with someone else.'

Izram, intrigued, had to struggle to maintain his act of cold detachment. 'How d'you know?' he asked, still gazing into the mid-distance.

Lan explained. He recalled the previous

night's telephone conversation, and Spinner's change of tone. Spinner had said 'eight-thirty' too, and wasn't that more likely to refer to evening arrangements than morning? He told Izram, convinced now that he was right.

Izram was silent for a moment. Then he said, still without looking at Lan, 'Are you going to apologise for saying that I deliberately missed a catch?'

Lan knew he hadn't said that and he baulked at making a major admission of guilt. On the other hand, he hated being at cross purposes with his best friend. So, carefully and sincerely, he said, 'I know you'd never ever do that, Iz.'

Honour thus being satisfied, Izram signified his change in mood by leaping on Lan and pushing him under the water. Lan retaliated by grabbing Izram's legs and pulling *him* under. They emerged gasping, friends again.

'So what can we do?' Izram asked. 'We can't make Grace marry him if she doesn't want to.'

'We can make her want to.'

'How?'

'By helping him look a bit groovier. He needs to shape up and get with it, like Paul McCartney and Mick Jagger.'

Izram looked doubtful.

'It's just clothes and haircut,' Lan said.

Izram thought it might be a bit more than

that, otherwise any old fusspot — even Mr Thistleton — could transform himself into a vintage rock star overnight. But he was willing to agree that Spinner's general appearance could benefit from a rigorous makeover. 'We made a start,' he said. 'We bought him that cool tie today.'

'Maybe we should give it to him now,' Lan mused. 'I bet he hasn't brought anything decent with him.'

'You crazy? Why should we give him a new tie when he's going off to meet someone who's not Grace? We don't want him marrying a Melburnian! He'd move here and we'd never see him again.'

'Sorry, I didn't think of that.' Lan thought of it now. The situation seemed grim. 'Of course,' he said, looking for a glimmer of hope, 'he might not be meeting a *girl*friend. I only guessed he was. All he said was he was going to a friend's place, an old friend he hadn't seen for a long time.'

'That's sure to mean a lady,' Izram said. 'He'd say "mate" if it was a man.'

'How can we find out for sure?'

'We could just ask him.'

Lan shook his head. 'I did and he wouldn't say. He got very grumpy. It was hard enough to make him leave a phone number.'

Izram's brow cleared. 'We've got a number? Then we'll ring and see who answers.'

They left it until just before lights out. Lan dialled the number. It rang maybe a half dozen times before it was picked up. A female voice said, 'Hello'.

Lan covered the handpiece. 'It *is* a lady!' he whispered to Izram. 'Um, who's speaking?'

'Who is *this* speaking?'

That had got him nowhere. 'Is Mr McGinty there, please?'

'Yes, he is. I'll just get him.'

'No, don't bother,' Lan said quickly. 'Could you give him a message, please? Tell him everything's OK, nobody drowned, and everyone's in bed. Thanks. Bye.'

He hung up.

'What did she sound like?' Izram asked.

Lan shrugged. 'All right, I guess. Nice. I dunno.'

They looked at each other. 'What are we going to do?' Izram asked.

Lan yawned. 'Now? Go to bed. We'll think about it in the morning.'

Twelve

Captain's Diary Saturday 20 January (morning)

I woke up early. My head was full of cricket. I suppose this is one of the prices you pay for being captain. There is always something to think about or a problem to fix. Mr Howard said once that the job of being Australian cricket captain was more important than that of being Prime Minister. It is so true. He has other people to run the country for him and make all the decisions while he flies about having his photo taken and watching cricket and enjoying himself, but being captain is a hands-on responsibility. Without John Howard Australia would survive, but where would we be without Steve Waugh?

More Sam-Izram problems. It would be better if Sam joined in things more, like the swimming yesterday, because that builds team spirit. But he came down for the barbecue and was friendly enough, although I noticed Izram kept staring at him in a pretty unfriendly way. Actually, I wasn't really sure whether it was a good idea to mix so much with the other teams, especially those that we'd be playing against soon. Spinner said this was taking things a bit too seriously. I wanted to say, 'What if you had to play against that old friend you had dinner with last night?' but then I remembered that the old friend was a lady and that would never happen. But it is the same situation.

For instance, the Dead Reds are playing the Tasmanian Tigers today. I asked Jermaine how they could be Aboriginal if they had fair hair and he said it probably went back a long way — they could have a white grandparent or great-grandparent. He pointed to a Dead Red called Kevin who also has fair skin. His grandfather was white and worked on a cattle station but after Kevin's father was born the family had been split up and Kevin's father, who was not even three years old, was taken away. I asked who had taken him away and Jermaine said 'Government people'. He never saw his mother again and it was years and years later that he found out he had brothers and sisters. It was a very sad story and Jermaine said it wasn't unusual. He too has people in his extended family who were taken away as children. So now, if I have to bowl to Kevin and Jermaine, I might think about those stolen children and feel sorry, and I might go a bit soft, like I did in the game against the Hunters. I think it must be easier to play aggressively if you don't like or know anything about the other team.

Jermaine said, 'In the bush we always know our mob. But in the city, people say to blokes like Kevin, "Ah, but you're not a real Aborigine".' I told him it was like what people say to us nips: 'But you're not a real Australian' — even the ones who were born here or have an Australian-born parent. I told him my parents came from Vietnam and Andy told him he was Malaysian Chinese, and Hiroki said his father was Japanese. Jermaine seemed surprised. He said, 'I thought you all nips, all the same.'

Jermaine said that they come from different 'clans' or tribes. (Like yesterday, we were playing on the traditional land of the Wurundjeri.) He wrote his down for me: his father is Wangkunurra from the Simpson Desert and his mother is Anyakidinya from northern South Australia. He said to me, 'Do you speak Vietnamese?' and I said 'Yes,' and he said, 'What's the Vietnamese for lbw then?' and I said, 'lbw' and he laughed. Then he told me this good joke: The spider walks to the crease. 'Oh not, not him!' says the grasshopper. 'Is he good?' asks the beetle. 'It's not that,' says the grasshopper. 'It's just that he stays in so long. The only way to get him out is llllbw.'

He's quite friendly, but I'm a bit nervous of him. It's sometimes hard to tell if he is joking or serious, like in the bus yesterday when I thought for a minute he was going to bite me. Also — and I didn't know this before our tour of the MCG — Aborigines have been pretty good cricketers. The first Australian cricket team to visit England was Aboriginal. They played forty-seven matches in 1868: won fourteen, drew nineteen, lost fourteen. (The first white team that went to England ten years later wasn't as good.) We saw a photo of them at the MCG. I liked some of the names: Dick-a-Dick, Mosquito, Red Cap, and King Cole. And in the 1930s an Aboriginal fast bowler called Eddie Gilbert who played for Queensland was famous. He used to send them down like greased lightning. Once he bowled Don Bradman for a duck and knocked the bat out of his hand! Jermaine said he didn't know about any of that either. I could see that it made him proud and it's sure to inspire all the Aboriginal teams so we'll have to watch out.

This is the second day and I'm not sure I'm acclimatised yet. It would be easier if Melbourne had a climate but Spinner says it just has weather. And that keeps changing. How do people in Melbourne know what to wear? Yesterday started off grey and cool, and then the sun came out and it got so hot we took off our tops. Then later it rained a bit, and last night it was warm and still and we went to bed with the fan on but then a wind blew all the curtains and I got up and turned it off. Today it is hot again. So far. Spinner says there's a famous joke: If you don't like the weather in Melbourne, wait ten minutes.

As a joke, it's not very funny but it is certainly true.

Six months ago it was the Nips,
who are they?
Today it's the Nips, wow, look at
them play!
We bat with fire and we bowl with
guts,
We drive all the other teams
totally nuts.

Andy Chen

Team Meeting — The Captain's Notes

Harmony Cup, Saturday, Day Two

Our effort yesterday was great and we got results (and momentum). Today will be tougher: 25 overs and a more experienced team. Plus the Dragons are local and they'll have the crowd on their side. Let's put them under pressure!

- Bowlers: do early damage
- Batsmen: doesn't matter how far down the order you're batting, go out there and do your best for the team.
- Remember what Spinner says: The harder you work the luckier you get.
- Remember that the great Ricky Ponting wished us good luck and said he hoped we would win. We are the only team in the competition to have the support of a Test player!

Thirteen

Lan's last ball of the last over clipped the batsman's pad and hit the stumps via the inside edge of the bat. The batsman looked surprised. Lan and the fielders leapt in the air in jubilation: it was the perfect finish to what had been a hard-fought innings.

'Well done, Nips,' said Spinner, when they came off, 'but don't start countin' yer chickens. You've got 128 to beat after lunch, so steer clear of the curry and watermelon.'

They grinned. It was a reminder of the lavish luncheon spread that had helped to lay low the King's XI in their match against them last year.

They joined the queue in the pavilion.

'I don't see any curry and watermelon,' Sam said, surveying the buffet.

Lan explained the reference and Sam's hand hesitated over the pieces of barbecued chicken.

'Maybe I'll just have a sandwich.'

'Nah, go for it. That's one advantage of losing the toss. It's a lot easier batting after lunch than fielding.'

'Especially if you're not an opener.'

Lan looked at him. 'Does it worry you, being an opener?'

'No. But I think it worries Izram.'

Lan looked around, but Izram was on another line, helping himself to a drink. Nevertheless, he lowered his voice. 'It shouldn't. He's usually third bat. He was only moved up for a game or two when we lost David. But then we got you.'

'Yeah. Exactly.'

'Exactly what?'

'That's the reason he doesn't like me.'

Lan could hardly argue that Sam was wrong, that Izram *did* like him, since the opposite was more obvious each day. But as captain, he had to do everything he could to avoid friction in the team. He said, 'I dunno what's bothering Iz, but I don't think it's that. He wanted you on the team, Sam, we all did. But Iz knows more about the game than any of us, and he respects and admires skill. So whatever his problem is, it's nothing to do with where or how you play. He rates you high.'

Sam said nothing and they loaded their plates and took them outside to the tables. But when they were seated Sam said quietly, 'You're a good captain, Lan.'

'Am I?' Lan said, pleased and wanting to hear more. 'I'm never sure what makes a good captain. Spinner says the skin of a rhino and the patience of a saint.'

'Well, for one thing, you stay calm. That's good for the team because if the captain's not upset and he's saying it's all OK then you feel the game's under control. And you keep the team together and make everyone believe in their own ability.'

'Thanks.' Lan glowed with pleasure. He thought it was easily the nicest thing anyone had ever said to him. 'What's your captain like then — the team you play with back home?'

'The team I used to play with? All right, I guess. But not a very good motivator. During team talks I used to switch off, but with you I really listen because you usually have something interesting to say. And our captain would never have got us writing poems, not in a million years.'

'I pinched that idea from Steve Waugh,' Lan admitted.

'He probably pinched it from someone else. The point is, we wrote them. And we sing that team song and I reckon it helps our game.'

'I think so, too.'

'What helps your game?' It was Jermaine, looming above them and swigging from a bottle of water.

'As if we'd tell you,' Lan said.

Jermaine wiped his mouth with the back of his hand and grinned. 'Don't matter, we'll still clean you Nips up. If you win today, that is. I heard it was tough this morning.'

'Then you heard wrong,' Lan said calmly.

'We're on track to win,' Sam said.

Jermaine regarded him through narrow eyes. 'You a slogger or a bowler?'

'Both,' said Sam.

'What number d'ya bat?'

'Sam's our opener,' Lan said.

'You're a slogger then. I reckon I'll pitch the first ball about this far outside the off and take your leg stump.' Jermaine held his hands about a half-metre apart.

Sam didn't blink. 'You can try. But I oughta warn you: those are my favourites. I smash 'em for six.'

'Quack, quack!' Jermaine grinned. 'Watch out tomorrow, Nips!' He headed into the pavilion.

'The only way you Dead Heads will win the Cup is if they raffle it!' Andy called after him. 'And even then you'll have to buy all the tickets!'

Some of the Nips at the table laughed but Lan shook his head. 'Cool it, Andy.'

'Why? Did ya hear what he said to Sam?'

'He was only joking.'

'So was I.'

'It didn't sound like joking. It sounded like sledging. Don't call them Dead Heads.'

'It's only sledging if it's on the field. Isn't that right, Iz?'

'Um ... yeah, I think so.'

'Off-field, it's called mental domination,' Andy said. 'It's all about making the opposition feel like losers.'

'That's why he quacked at Sam. Now when Sam faces up to the bowler he'll worry about getting out for a duck,' Izram explained.

'No I won't,' said Sam forcefully. 'It takes more than that to put me off my stroke. Maybe it works better on wicket-keepers.'

'Well, whatever you call it,' Lan said quickly, seeing Izram's furious look, 'we can feel good about ourselves without putting down the other side. Remember Macca and his two blond mates sledging us that first day at the cricket club? Remember how we felt?' Lan certainly did. He remembered the 'Can't catch, can't bowl' taunt from one, and the other's implication that you had to be white to bowl for Australia. He remembered putting his arm around Izram and telling him not to let it get to him.

Izram obviously remembered it too. 'I wasn't saying sledging was a good thing,' he said earnestly. 'I was just explaining how it worked.'

'How what works?' asked Spinner, shambling up with a plate piled high with a riotous mix of food. He sat down and began to attack a drumstick with relish.

'Nothing,' said Lan. They all knew Spinner's views on sledging. In an attempt to steer him in a different direction, he said, 'Didya have a nice dinner last night, Spinner?'

'I did. And it certainly set my mind at rest to get your phone call just as I was sittin' down to it.'

Lan nodded. 'I thought you might be worried about us.'

'Nah, not with you in charge, Captain.'

Spinner licked the chicken bone clean, picked up his fork and started on the potato salad. 'This is good tucker,' he said.

'Grace is a terrific cook,' Lan said.

Spinner looked at him. 'WG? What brought that on?'

'I just remembered. She made you that

Christmas cake, didn't she? I bet she makes good potato salad too.'

'Someone pass me the salt,' Spinner said.

Izram pushed it across the table. 'I expect she's missing us all.'

'What, after two days? She'll hardly know we've gone.'

'You oughta phone her,' Lan said.

'What for?'

Did Spinner need a reason? Lan couldn't think of one. He looked across at Izram for help.

'To find out how Larri is,' Izram said, inspired.

'I bet he's missing you like *mad*!' Lan said. It occurred to him almost immediately that this might not be viewed as a desirable state, so he added quickly, 'It's lucky he loves Grace so much, otherwise he might've pined away when you left.'

'Yeah, dogs don't like staying with strangers,' Izram said, with heavy emphasis on the last word.

Spinner wiped his plate with a piece of bread. He looked at them both. 'What are you two gabbin' about? Go and get more tucker if your tongues need somethin' to do.'

'Did you have some good tucker last night, Spinner?' Lan asked.

'A nice old-fashioned baked dinner and a chocolate sponge pudding,' Spinner said. 'Came home full as a goog.'

At the end of the table, Tomas pricked up his ears. He'd had some trouble following this conversation but he thought he recognised that word. 'Do you know how you say 'googly' in Spanish?' he said eagerly. 'It's *servidor de googly*.'

They all laughed.

'You're turning into a real international cricketer, Onya,' Lan said.

Tomas beamed. In a little over six months, Tomas's life had been transformed. From the isolation of the non-English-speaking outfield, he'd been scooped up and hurled into the thick of the game. Sometimes the pace of it left him dazed, but the security and fun of being part of a team was something he treasured, and Lan was his special hero.

He'd woken up early this morning, long before the seven o'clock call, and had caught Lan practising shots in front of the mirror.

'Don't tell anyone,' Lan had said.

'Why no tell?'

'It's not cool. They might think I'm up myself. Andy will laugh.'

Tomas didn't see why it was funny. He was going to get up early tomorrow morning and practise in front of the mirror, too.

Spinner looked at his watch. 'Orright, mateys, time to go. Play hard and remember the rules: no sledging, accept the umpire's decision, no arguments, no backchat, no dirty looks. I'll be watchin'. Make me proud.'

It was what the old coach always said, and they all understood what it meant. Making Spinner proud had nothing to do with winning and everything to do with how they played.

'Good luck, Akka. Good luck, Sam. Smash 'em for six!' Lan gave them a pat on the back and watched as they padded up and walked out to the crease.

The Dragons' captain set his field. The seagulls abandoned the pavilion and flew in to take up their positions.

'Why are seagulls so interested in cricket?' Lan asked. 'D'you remember all the gulls on Adelaide Oval? And they're here, too. It's not as if we're near the beach.'

'They always hang around the wicket,' Izram said. 'You'd think they'd fly around where people are eating.'

'There's a theory,' said Spinner, 'that when cricketers die they come back as seagulls. That's why they squat near the wicket.'

Lan looked at the birds with renewed interest. There was a big fat one strutting at mid-on as if he owned the pitch. That was probably W.G. Grace.

Fourteen

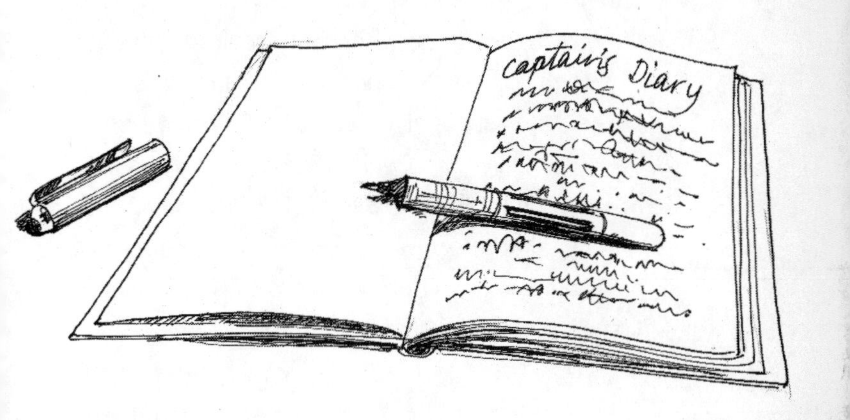

Captain's Diary Saturday 20 January (late)

We are into the finals! Tomorrow it will be the Nips up against the Dead Reds. Everyone played well today and some played extra well. Our momentum is fantastic!

After lunch we were chasing 126. Sam and Akram opened the batting and soon had runs on the board, but it was Sam who slaughtered the bowling. He reached his forty in just thirty-two balls. Again and again the ball scorched across the grass, always going just where the fielder wasn't. He and Akka batted well together but Akka was caught behind in his fourth over for thirteen, and then Iz came in and when Sam retired not out it was my turn. Together Iz and I added forty-three to the total before his wicket went. I was on thirty-eight when I went for a hook but I gloved the ball to the wicket-keeper — a bit unlucky, because I'd hooked a similar ball to the boundary in the previous over. I think this time I was through the shot too soon. Anyway, our top order got 3/106, which relieved the pressure on the others. And at the end of our innings we were 5/127.

One of the good things about this carnival is that everyone gets lots of chances to play and improve their game. The teams who lost matches in the first round aren't totally eliminated: they play each other and accumulate points, and in between there are coaching clinics. (Rikki has been to a couple of these.) So Russell is feeling pretty cheerful, even though the Hunters have no chance at all of winning the Cup.

We were watching a cricket video last night and I was explaining tactics to him. I said, 'See, Warnie's bowling these little tiddlies and the batsman can't get any runs. Some people would reckon that's pretty boring cricket, right? But see what happens: after five of the tiddlies, Warnie suddenly bowls a good straight one and the batsman's so fed up he whacks it hard towards mid-field and he's caught, he's out.'

Later, Russell said to me, 'I like cricket but I really didn't love it until I met you. I didn't understand it, but you've taught me a lot of things.' So that made me feel good, because it was how I was in the beginning, before I met Spinner.

Tonight after dinner we saw a bit of Melbourne. Mr Warton went with us and we caught a tram and got out near the Flinders Street Station. This is enormous, with a huge green dome on top and a red-and-orange-striped clock-tower. It reminded me of the towers that Linh and Tien build in Lego and for a moment I missed them and felt home-sick.

The streets were full of cars and trams and taxis, and there were people everywhere. Russell said there were more people at the station than in the whole of the Tiwi Islands!

A lot of the Hunters had never seen a big city before and Mr Warton got very worried whenever we had to cross a road. I got a bit worried too, because before we left, one of the Dragons, who lives in Melbourne, warned me that you mustn't tread on the tramlines in the city because they are live and you'll get a shock. He said that sometimes, when the current is flowing really strongly, like on a Saturday night, you could even be electrocuted. He said he knew a boy who had been killed this way.

So at first we were really careful and hopped over all the tracks but then we noticed that other people were stepping on them and not being electrocuted. Phon said maybe Melburnians had built up immunity over the years, or maybe they knew the times when the strong current was switched on, but nobody was game to touch a track to find out. When we got back I told Spinner about the Dragon's warning and he laughed and said, 'And I s'pose he told you the Yarra flows upside down too?' So I knew then it had been a joke. I'll have to think of some way to pay that Dragon back.

I liked the area called Southbank. The

river did look brown and sludgy, like it was flowing upside down, but as it got darker and the lights came on it looked very pretty. And with all the ferry boats and flags and banners waving and people strolling and sitting at cafes and music playing it was an exciting place to be. We bought barbecued sweet corn and satays and watched a man tied up in chains get himself free. He took less than ninety seconds. We all clapped and some people in the crowd threw him money. Then we walked along by the river and a scruffy man sitting on the footpath with a lot of plastic bags asked Mr Warton if he could spare a few dollars for his bus fare. Mr Warton said he couldn't. I thought the man might be hungry so I offered him my sweet corn — there was more than half of it left — but he just looked at me and said, 'Piss off, kid,' so I ate it myself. Other beggars were drawing pictures on the pavement with coloured chalk and asking people for money. It must be like this in India, except of course there are no cows in the streets here.

When we got back to St Paul's we had a quick team meeting and now I am writing this. The meeting went very well. There was a lot of positive input. We all enjoyed the visit to Southbank and are looking forward to the match tomorrow. Mr Thistleton sent a message wishing us luck and saying he would come and watch. He also wrote us a motivational poem which I read out, but none of us knew what 'gird your loins' means. Akka said Mr Warton had probably copied it down wrong and it should have said 'guard your lions'. I suppose it's one of those funny cricketing terms (like 'popping crease' and 'silly mid-on') that means 'guard your wicket' or something. (Andy has a joke about a popping crease that is hilarious but it is too rude to include here.)

After the meeting, Hiroki told me that he can't sleep. He said, 'As soon as I shut my eyes I see fast bowlers charging towards me.' I don't know why he's so worried: we haven't had any real quickies. But perhaps what is a medium-pacer to me is a thunderbolt to Roki. I tried to reassure him but the truth is, he's an accident waiting to happen. Even with his lenses he doesn't see too well and he can't walk from one side of the room to the other without knocking into something. He's not twelve yet and he's already broken his arm three times. I thought if anyone got injured on this trip it would be him, but so far, so good. He only has to get through one more match. He says he hates fielding, but he just lacks confidence in his ability to catch and throw a ball accurately.

I'm more worried about Sam. He's playing so well yet he still seems tense. Perhaps he's not enjoying the trip. At first I put it down to the shyness that anyone would feel if he was suddenly chucked into the middle of a team of friends, but now I think it's more than that. There's something on his mind. It's no good talking about it with Izram and it's no good asking Spinner either, because he doesn't notice things like that. As a coach, he'll pick up the smallest change in your technique but he's not so observant when it comes to people and how they might be feeling. (Grace is an example of this. If they've had a fight he should definitely ring her, especially since she is minding his dog while he is seeing another woman!)

Perhaps there's some family problem that's bothering Sam. His sister did give me her phone number, as if she expected something might come up. Whatever it is, I hope it stays away at least until after the match tomorrow.

The battle for the Cup is about
to start,
Gird your loins, bat bravely and
play from the heart.
You've done all the hard work,
now give it your best,
When you're on the train home is
the time to rest.

Reginald Thistleton

Fifteen

Lan hovered indecisively over the buffet. Go for it, he told himself; this is your chance to try Coco Pops. When you're in foreign places, he told himself, you should eat foreign foods. He knew, of course, that Coco Pops weren't unique to Melbourne — you could buy them in supermarkets back home — but they were a foreign food to him. It had taken him years to persuade his mother to buy Vegemite — she'd only just given in on that — but the chances of Coco Pops ever being added to the Nguyen breakfast menu seemed remote in the extreme. So here was a golden opportunity.

On the other hand — and this was what was really holding him back — yesterday at breakfast, and before the addition of Coco Pops to the buffet, he had eaten Weetbix. And so far this morning he had got out of bed on the same side and at the same time as yesterday; he had showered and cleaned his teeth in the same way; he was wearing exactly the same clothes he had worn yesterday. Was it worth risking the Harmony Cup for a bowl of Coco Pops? To be on the safe side, he should have the same breakfast as yesterday.

He was reaching for the Weetbix when Izram materialised at his side.

'Come back upstairs,' he said in a low urgent voice. 'I've got something to show you.'

'What, now? Can't it wait till after breakfast?'

'No. It has to be now, while everyone's down here.'

'Why? What's the big secret?'

'I can't tell you, I have to show you.'

'If it's about Spinner's present, we've —'

'It's not about that. C'mon, Lan, hurry. This is important.'

'Oh, all right.' A rather disgruntled Lan followed Izram out of the dining room and up the stairs. 'I was trying to keep everything the same,' he said. 'You know, so our luck would hold and we'd win again. If all the Weetbix is gone when I get back —'

'Everything's not the same. There's been a big change.'

Izram's tone was so portentous that Lan looked at him in some trepidation. What had happened upstairs? Had someone drowned in the bathtub? Fallen out of a window? Died in his sleep? His heart momentarily stopped, and then he recalled seeing Spinner in the dining room, tucking into his usual mountain of bacon and eggs. So, not him. Besides, there was an air of suppressed excitement about Izram that seemed to indicate that, whatever surprise awaited Lan upstairs, it was not something that had particularly traumatised his wicket-keeper.

'What sort of change?' he demanded.

'Wait.' Izram opened the door of their room and they went in. Lan's eyes darted around. Everything looked normal. Was the body in the bathroom then?

'Shut the door,' Izram said. He walked over to Sam's bed in the far corner, knelt down and pulled a soft-sided bag from under it.

'What are you doing?' Lan demanded, surprised.

Izram didn't answer. He started to unzip the bag.

'Hey, that's Sam's bag! Leave it alone, Iz.'

'Come over here and take a look.'

Disturbed but curious, Lan shut the door and

went over. Izram pulled out an item of clothing and shoved it in his hands. 'What's that?'

Lan looked. It was a pair of underpants. Bikini underpants. Pale pink bikini underpants. With a dinky little bow in the middle of the narrow waist-band.

Lan blinked. He sat down on the bed. 'Whose are these?' he said stupidly.

'They're in Sam's bag, aren't they?'

'Sam wears pink underpants?'

'And blue ones. And plain old white.' Izram pulled out two more pairs and shoved them at Lan.

'Why does he wear girl's underpants?' Lan still didn't get it.

'Because he *is* a girl, you dicko! She's always been a girl. She's been fooling us all along!'

Lan was speechless. It couldn't be true. He'd never suspected such a thing, not once. Nobody had. He looked at the underpants again. Was there another explanation? He couldn't think of one that made any sort of sense. 'Are there any more girl's clothes in the bag?'

Izram shook his head. 'Only unisex T-shirts and tanks and jeans and stuff. These were hidden in an inside pocket.'

'You shouldn't have been going through some-one's bag. Jeez, Iz!'

'Good thing I did. We'd never have known otherwise.'

And now that they did? What now? Lan's mind was still churning with the implications.

'I told you there was something funny about him — I mean her,' Izram said. 'But you wouldn't listen.' He sat back on his heels, an unmistakeable look of triumph on his face.

This was a bit much. 'You never had a clue, Iz, admit it! You just didn't like Sam.'

'I did have a clue,' Izram said stubbornly. 'At the MCG. I tried to tell you then.'

'What happened at the MCG?'

'It was when you went back to the pitch. We were on our way back to the entrance and the guide pointed out the toilets and told us about the MCG shop. About half the group went into the loo but Sam went off to the shop. I hung around in the underpass waiting for you and after a while when everybody had gone I saw Sam coming back — he looked around but he didn't see me — and started to head into the Ladies. I didn't think, I just thought she'd made a mistake, and I called out, "Hey dicko, if you can't see that sign you need glasses!" and she stopped and turned bright red and scuttled off into the Men's.'

Lan noted how Izram switched between 'he' and 'she' when referring to Sam, but he was feeling just as confused. 'Did you go in too?'

Izram shook his head. 'It didn't hit me until later. I was still there when he ... she came out and she muttered something like, "Thanks, that would've been embarrassing," but, you know, those signs were so clear and I really thought there must be something wrong with his eyesight that he didn't want anyone to know about. That's what I was gonna tell you. It wasn't till afterwards I remembered how she'd looked around her as she was heading for the Ladies. I thought she was looking for you, but after, I wondered if she hadn't just been checking that the coast was clear. And then I realised that I'd never once, during this whole trip, seen Sam using a bathroom or a toilet.'

Lan realised he hadn't either. He remembered the first night when Sam had locked the bathroom door and then emerged, ready for bed in striped pyjamas. He recalled her up and fully dressed before anyone else in the room had awoken.

'Then there was all that stuff she knew about women's cricket,' Izram went on. 'Sam said she was interested because her sister played cricket, but then I thought back to when her sister brought Sam to our match —'

'And told us she knew practically nothing about cricket!' Lan exclaimed. Why hadn't he picked up on that? And other things were occurring to him. Sam's refusal to go swimming, for one.

I don't like swimming ... She'd told him on the train how much she enjoyed the sport. How had he missed that?

'Why didn't you say something earlier?' he asked.

Izram looked at him indignantly. 'You told me to leave off Sam, that it was bad for team morale! You said I had Sam on the brain. You said you didn't want to hear any more about him. So I thought I'd better get some proof first.'

They both looked at the underpants. 'I'll kill her!' Izram exclaimed. 'What about all the times we've undressed in front of her?'

'I'm not sure there were so many times. I never caught her looking, anyway. Remember that first night how she came out of the bathroom and got into bed and turned her back? You thought she was being unfriendly. And I don't think she ever used the change room at Bulleen, did she?'

'Who knows what she's seen,' Izram said grimly.

'Why d'you think she did it?'

'To get the trip to Melbourne. What else?'

'I guess.' Would *he* go to such lengths, Lan asked himself. Not if it involved impersonating a girl. But the whole idea was ludicrous. He'd never be able to pull off such a stunt — would any boy? (would any boy want to?) — but Sam had been almost totally successful. Even now, he had trouble getting his head around the gender swap, not to mention the possible consequences. 'So what do we do now?' he asked.

'Confront her,' Izram said.

'And after she's admitted it? What do we do then?'

'Chuck her off the team, of course.'

'Right before we play the final? Our best strokeplayer? Great move, Iz.'

'You think we shouldn't say anything? Just pretend we don't know she's a girl?'

'It's one option. This time yesterday we didn't know, and she played and we won.' *But it's different today*, a little voice inside him said. *Today you do know.*

Izram said, 'Well, will we say something to Sam or not?'

The door suddenly opened. They turned.

'Say what to me?' Sam said. She saw the guilt on their faces and then the open bag at Izram's feet. They all stared at each other.

'Oh boy!' she said softly.

Sixteen

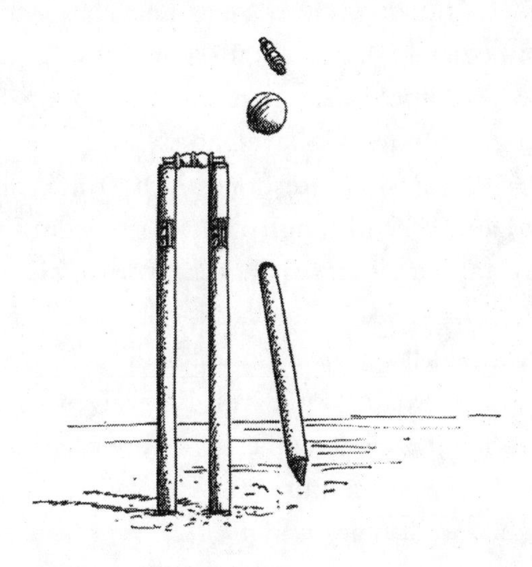

Sam advanced into the room and snatched the underpants from Lan's hands. She threw them into her bag, zipped it up and kicked it under her bed. 'So what are you going to do?' she said.

It was a good question but Lan didn't feel up to answering it immediately. He had a few of his own first. 'What made you do it?' he asked. 'Didn't you think you'd be found out?'

'No. I thought I had a good chance of getting away with it. None of you twigged when I met you that first Saturday.' She crossed her arms across her chest and looked at them defiantly. 'I haven't done anything to be ashamed of. Unlike you two, snooping about in a person's private property.'

The discomfort that Lan had been feeling immediately doubled, but Izram was outraged.

'If you'd been honest with us from the beginning, we wouldn't have had to!'

'How was I dishonest? Did I lie?' She looked at Lan. 'When I rang you after the radio show, did I say anything that wasn't totally honest?'

Lan tried to recall. 'No. But you didn't say you were a girl!'

'If I had, would you have given me a try-out and invited me to come to Melbourne?'

'No,' he admitted.

'Well, that's why I did it.'

'Hang on,' said Izram. 'You did lie. You told us your name was Sam. What's your real name? What did you put on those forms you had to sign?'

'I put my name, Sam Chin Po. And I didn't lie! Sam is my family name and in China it comes first.'

'But in *Australia*,' said Izram, with heavy emphasis, 'you're Chin Po Sam.'

She shrugged. 'Would it have made any difference? Anyway, everybody at school calls me Sam.'

Lan looked at her curiously. 'Do you look like this at school?'

She pulled a wry face and ran her fingers

through her short crop. 'No, this is a Nips special. I had my hair cut right after our phone call. And I trimmed my nails and got some boy's clothes. That's about all. I haven't exactly got a figure that gives me away.'

'But you didn't go swimming,' Lan said.

'No way!' Sam grinned.

Lan couldn't help admiring the way she was handling the situation. It was how she played cricket: with attack rather than defence, and no show of fear. 'Do you play in a girls' team at home?' he asked.

Sam shook her head.

'Why not?'

'Aren't any. Not in my school, anyway.'

'Were you the only girl?'

She grinned. 'The only girl in the whole inter-school competition. You should have seen the opposition when I walked out to bat in my first game. They were like, *It's a girl!*'

'Yeah well, that's what they'll say this morning when we tell them the truth about you,' said Izram.

'So don't tell them,' Sam said.

Izram and Lan looked at each other.

'Does anyone else know?' Sam asked.

Lan shook his head. 'Iz only told me ten minutes ago. He's the one who found you out.'

Sam flicked him a look. 'Mr Detective. You followed me to the toilets, didn't you?'

'No, I didn't, so there. But it made me suspicious when you went into the wrong one.'

'But nothing else did?' Sam asked. 'Nothing in the way I batted or bowled or fielded made either of you suspect me?'

'No,' Lan said.

'Not really,' Izram admitted.

'That's because there's no difference between men's and women's cricket. Same game, same skills. If you don't tell anyone I'm a girl they'll never pick it.' She looked at them both and said passionately, 'Let me play and we can win this match today. How about it?'

Izram glanced at Lan. Ultimately, it was his decision.

Lan hesitated. 'I'm not sure it's right.'

'Why not? In what way?' Sam demanded.

'It might be against the rules, for one thing.'

'It can't be, otherwise I wouldn't have been allowed to play in inter-schools competition.'

'She's got a point,' Izram said. 'Why don't we find out? Spinner will know — or Laura Jolly. We can just ask in a casual sort of way whether a girl in the team would be against the rules. We don't have to say anything about Sam.'

Lan thought a question like that just before

a match might very well make Laura and Spinner very suspicious indeed. But he said, 'What if it is against the rules?'

'Then we dump Sam and play Rikki.'

'But Iz, we won't be allowed to play at all!' Lan pointed out. 'Not if we've broken the rule in our previous matches. The Nips will be disqualified from the competition. Do you want to risk it?'

'I hadn't thought of that,' Izram said. 'OK, not a word to Spinner or Laura then.'

'Well, here's the next scenario,' Lan said. 'We keep quiet and Sam plays and we win the match and then we find out it's against the rules. What do we do: confess and hand the Cup back, or stay quiet and know we didn't win it totally honestly?'

There was a brief silence.

'It's not really dishonest, is it?' Sam said, and there was a note of pleading in her voice. 'Not like lying about a catch or a nick, or tampering with the ball.'

'It's still lying,' Lan said unhappily. 'You've pretended to be a boy. If it turns out to be against the rules, how could we keep the Cup? I'm really sorry, Sam, but —'

'Before you definitely make up your mind,' she interrupted, 'will you let me tell you exactly why I did this?'

Lan looked at his watch. 'Make it quick.'

'Thanks.' She perched on the end of the bed, facing him. 'I've been crazy about cricket ever since my first Have-A-Go coaching clinic. I cried when I thought I couldn't play in a team but I was lucky, the school agreed I could play with the boys. I didn't tell my parents, they would've had a fit.' She noted Lan's expression. 'Yeah, I do have parents. They're very traditional Chinese, especially my mother. Ping-pong is OK, and swimming. Nice traditional Chinese sports. But cricket? And playing with boys? Anyway, my older sister Nin — you met her — took me to and from games and kept the secret. She approved: she said girls ought to be able to do whatever they wanted to, especially if they were good at it. Then I read about you in the paper last year —'

'The story about Spinner and our match against King's?' Lan said.

Sam nodded. 'That was another thing. I wasn't just the only girl in my team, I was the only nip. Everyone else was Anglo. And then I read about your team, Nips XI, and how you'd started it and found this fantastic coach, an ex-Test player. I was like, they'll be learning so much! I wish I could play with them. And then I heard you on the radio and it just sounded so exciting — the trip and the Cup competition and the ACB organising the whole thing. I thought, why can't they have something like that for girls? And then I thought, well, why don't

I be a boy, just for this trip? I won't get another chance. This time next year I'll probably look much more like a girl.'

Lan and Izram exchanged amused glances.

'I will! Just wait.'

'Were you planning to ever tell us you were a girl?' Izram asked.

'Oh yes. Of course. After the carnival. I thought if I'd played really well, you might invite me to join the Nips.'

'What did your sister think of this plan?' Lan asked.

'She thought you'd twig when we came that Saturday. When you didn't and she had to sign those forms, she was a bit worried about me going to Melbourne but she gave in. She's a real feminist. She doesn't believe in gender barriers. She says there was too much of that in China.'

'At the station she gave me a card with her phone numbers on it and told me to ring if anything happened,' Lan said. 'I know what she had in mind now.'

'She was like, what about the change room, how will you wash and shower, what happens if there's only one toilet? But I've been playing in a boys' team for a long time and it's never been a problem. It hasn't been a problem on this trip either, has it?'

'Well ... it might have been better if you'd had a separate room.'

'And stayed out of the change room!' Izram added.

'I didn't look,' Sam said. 'Honest!'

'Can I ask you something?' Izram asked.

'Sure.'

'Did you wear a box?'

Sam looked mischievous. 'Couldn't you tell?'

'No. I mean, I didn't really look. Anyway, your shirt was pretty long.' Izram's cheeks were pink.

Sam grinned. 'Maybe I did and maybe I didn't.'

There was the sound of voices in the corridor: breakfast was obviously coming to a close. Lan got to his feet. He'd been moved by Sam's ambition and initiative and the parallels with his own story. He wished he had more time to think about the problem, but he obviously had to make a decision now. And she was looking at him so hopefully. He felt terrible. 'Sam, I'm really sorry,' he said, 'but I think Rikki ought to play today instead of you.'

The door opened and Akram stuck his head in. 'So here you are! Lan, bad news.'

'What's up?'

Akram looked into the corridor behind him and lowered his voice. 'It's Andy. He's been sick all night and he's not much better now. I don't think he's up to playing today. He's in our room. You'd better come and see him.'

Lan looked at Izram in dismay. Without Sam in the team there was still a slim chance the Nips could win. Without both Sam *and* Andy, what were their chances?

Seventeen

Sam clutched Lan's arm, her face alive with renewed hope. 'This changes things, Lan! You really need me now.'

'Sam's right,' Izram began, and then, remembering Akram, lowered his voice. 'We won't win with both of them out of the team.'

'I don't know. You two wait here,' Lan said distractedly. What a morning of shocks this was turning out to be!

He left the room and accompanied Akram along the corridor. Ahead of them, a few boys ran in and out of rooms, talking and calling to each other, but most seemed to be still downstairs.

'Why didn't you say something earlier if Andy's been sick all night?' Lan asked.

'He wouldn't let me,' Akram replied. 'He said it was probably something he'd eaten and he'd be fine in the morning. But I don't reckon he is.'

'Did he go down to breakfast?'

'He hasn't left the room.'

Akram opened the door and the two of them went in. Andy, dressed in his team shirt and shorts, was sitting on the edge of his bed and making fumbling attempts to tie the laces of a sneaker on his left foot. It was like watching someone wearing batting gloves trying to thread a needle.

'I heard you had a bad night,' Lan said.

Andy glanced up, and Lan was shocked at the colour of his complexion and the shadowing under his eyes. 'Oh, hullo. I told Akka not to say anything.'

Lan sat down on the bed next to him. 'You don't look so good.'

'Nah, I'm OK. There's nothin' left inside me to come out. If I don't eat or drink I'll be all right.' Just the effort of speaking seemed to exhaust him.

'Akka said you think it might be something you ate last night.'

'Yeah. Maybe those chicken satays.'

'Has anybody else been sick?' Lan asked Akram.

'I don't think so. Nobody's said anything.'

'Let's hope they're all healthy then.' The match would have to be forfeited if they weren't, Lan calculated, and he would have to bear some of the blame. Steve Waugh would never let any of his players eat food from street vendors in foreign cities.

'Rikki's all right. I saw him at breakfast,' Akram said.

Mention of the twelfth man seemed to have a positive effect on Andy. 'I'm feeling better now,' he announced. Lan and Akram looked at him doubtfully. 'No, honest.' He smiled weakly and got to his feet. 'Where's my other shoe?'

'Here.' Akram handed it to him.

Andy reached for it, but suddenly clutched his stomach and grimaced. He sank back full length on the bed and groaned.

'Maybe we should get a doctor,' Lan said, worried.

'I'll … be … fine,' Andy muttered, his eyes closed and beads of sweat on his forehead.

'Well, you obviously can't play.'

'Yeah … can … soon.'

Lan looked at Akram. 'Go and get Spinner.'

While he waited, Lan ran through the various options in his mind, trying to decide what to do and in what order. Play Sam but not Rikki? Play Rikki but not Sam? Tell Spinner and Laura about Sam? Tell Spinner but not Laura? Tell the rest of the Nips? Tell nobody until after the match? Tell everybody before the match? He still hadn't come to a resolution by the time Spinner and Mr Warton appeared, Akram trailing in their wake.

'Oh dear,' said Mr Warton, wringing his hands in distress as he peered down at Andy lying limp and apparently lifeless on the bed. 'I wonder if it's a virus?'

Spinner looked at the patient too, and then sniffed the air. 'Crook guts,' he said.

'Pardon?'

'Runs at both ends. Probably somethin' he ate.'

Mr Warton turned almost as pale as Andy. 'Not here, I hope.'

'We think it might have been the satays at Southbank last night,' Lan said.

'Ah.' Mr Warton was visibly relieved. 'Well, we can fix that. I'll go and get the appropriate medication. That, plenty to drink, and a day in bed ought to see you right, young man.'

Any fight left in Andy seemed to have drained away. He shut his eyes and curled into a foetal position.

Spinner bent and removed Andy's shoe, and

then pulled the quilt over him. He took Lan aside. 'Better go and tell Rikki he's playing today. I'll stay here a while in case anything develops.'

'He's going to be all right, isn't he?'

'Andy? He'll be as fit as a Mallee bull tomorrow.'

'But we're leaving tonight.'

'We'll carry him onto the train if we have to. But my bet is he'll be back on his feet before then. Don't look so worried. Gettin' the runs is part of any cricket tour.'

Lan understood the pun but couldn't muster a grin. 'It'll be a tough match without Andy,' he said. *And without Sam*, he added to himself.

'It was always gunna be tough, matey. Those Dead Reds are good. But King's were good, too, and you came within a bull's roar in that match.'

The old man seemed to have bulls on the brain. Lan suddenly noticed that he was dressed rather more smartly than usual. His trousers were pressed and he was wearing a spotless blue shirt that Lan couldn't recall seeing before. 'You look nice, Spinner,' he said in surprise.

'Well, it's the final, isn't it? Bloke's gotta make an effort. I'm lookin' forward to seein' you get that Cup. Now listen: you got thirty-five overs and bowlers are restricted to seven overs each. Andy's out, so that means you and Sam, a spinner and a quickie. Bowl the maximum and try to take early wickets. You got Hiroki and Onya, right?'

Lan nodded. 'Akka, too, if we need him.' He hoped they wouldn't. Akka's bowling was on a par with Rikki's batting.

'That's up to you and Sam. You're the strongest bowlers. Now shake a leg and go and tell young Rikki here's his chance to show the ACB what he's made of.'

Lan bent over the bed. 'Seeya, Andy. Hope you get well soon.'

Andy opened one eye. 'Kill those Dead Reds,' he muttered, and lapsed into semi-consciousness.

Lan didn't have to go far to find his twelfth man. When he emerged from the room, Rikki was hovering nervously in the corridor. 'Is it true?' he asked. 'Andy's sick?'

Lan nodded. 'Looks like you'll get your chance to bat after all.'

Rikki's expression indicated that it was not a chance he'd been particularly praying for. Lan forced a note of cheerful optimism into his voice. 'Lucky for us you came, Rikki. And now you'll be able to go home and tell everybody you helped the Nips win the Harmony Cup.'

'I'm afraid I'll let you down, Lan.'

'Nah, you won't. You wouldn't be on the team if I thought you couldn't play.'

Rikki's face brightened. 'I'll try my best.'

'Great, Rikki. Now go and tell the others, will you? I have to get my things.

'Sure, Lan.' He sped off.

So where was he now in his pre-match strategy? Lan asked himself. Obviously, Andy's withdrawal would have a negative impact on the team. He couldn't compound it by suddenly springing on them the news that their best strokeplayer was a girl. Nor did it seem an appropriate time to go back and hit Spinner with the news; he could see Mr Warton trotting down the corridor towards him now.

He returned to his own room where Sam and Izram were anxiously awaiting him.

'It's bad news,' he said. 'Andy's out.' He gave them the details.

'And me?' Sam asked, looking at him in much the same way Linh and Tien looked at him when they wanted to come to after-school cricket practice.

He nodded. 'You can play. But it'll be tough, Sam. I need you in top form, batting *and* bowling.'

She played it cool, Lan noted. No cheers or whoops of triumph, just a quiet 'OK', but he didn't miss the gleam in her eye.

'Did you tell Spinner?' Izram asked.

Lan shook his head.

'Are you gonna tell anyone?' Sam asked.

'I've been thinking about that. It seems to me

that only one person really needs to know: the other captain.'

'Jermaine Miller? You're gonna tell *Jermaine*?' Izram seemed stunned.

Lan nodded. 'Yeah. If he's happy with it, fine.'

'And if he's not? What makes you think Jermaine will give us any advantage?'

'He's never seen Sam play. He's never seen any of us play. He's just as likely to rate her a disadvantage.' He looked at Sam. 'No offence.'

'That's OK. Plenty of guys think that way.'

'We'll show him, hey?' They grinned at each other.

'OK. Let's do it.' Unexpectedly, Izram grinned too.

Now that Sam stood revealed as a girl, Izram seemed to have got over his dislike, Lan reflected. Now why was that?

Eighteen

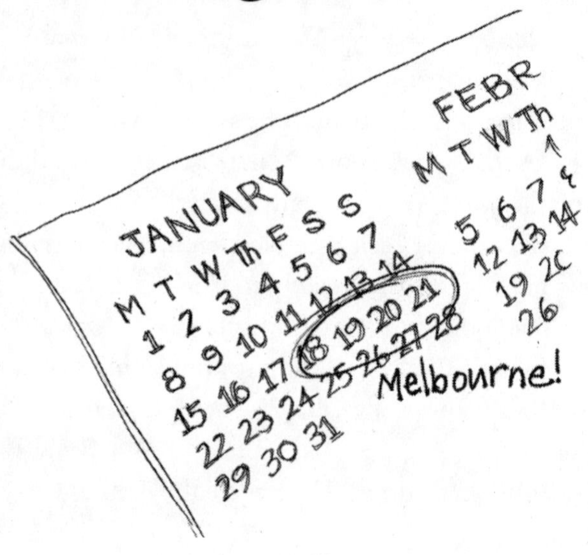

There was no chance for Lan to speak to Jermaine until after their arrival at the grounds, which were already buzzing with players and spectators eager to see the match that would decide the winners of the Harmony Cup. It was a magnificent day, the sky a brilliant blue with a slight breeze stirring the different national flags that hung from the veranda of the pavilion. Various sponsors had set up stands on the grassy areas outside and family groups were beginning to spread picnic blankets and set up tables and deckchairs. The event had even attracted, Lan discovered, a 'media presence' — at least, that was what the media liaison officer, the same young man who had stressed the importance of building momentum, called it.

'The ethnic press are here, of course, and they'll want to have a chat with you and perhaps one or two of your players from statistically significant migrant groups,' he explained to Lan, whom he'd waylaid between the changing room and the pavilion. 'Who would you suggest?'

'I'm not sure,' Lan said, looking around to see if he could spot Jermaine. 'What does that mean, statistically significant?'

'Well, Vietnamese or Chinese, for example. They're two big ethnic communities here in Melbourne.'

'There's me. I'm Australian-Vietnamese.'

'Great! And Chinese?'

'Well, there's —' Lan paused. Andy was back at St Paul's and not in a fit state to be interviewed by anyone and Sam certainly had a story to interest the press but right now was probably not the best time to tell it. 'We've got an Italian player,' he said brightly.

'I'm not sure the Italian press are here actually.'

'Why not?' asked Lan. 'Aren't they statistically significant? You seem to have a lot of Italian restaurants in Melbourne.'

'A lot of Chinese too. Any Chinese boys in your team?'

'Um, can these interviews wait until after the match?' Lan asked. 'It's, you know, a bit *distracting* for the players now.'

'Oh, absolutely! Just putting you in the picture. I'll tee things up. Where's Mr McGinty, by the way?'

'Someone's sick and he stayed behind. He'll be here later. You haven't seen Jermaine Miller, have you? The captain of the Dead Reds?'

'Ah, a *lot* of interest in that team! I did see some of them out on the pitch being photographed about five minutes ago ... Hang on, isn't he in that group over there?'

Lan looked towards the steps of the pavilion where Jermaine and a few other players were standing next to their coach, who seemed to be giving a press interview.

'Yeah, that's him. Thanks. Catch you later.'

'Good luck today!'

'Thanks.' Lan ran off, and as he approached the steps he could hear the coach of the Dead Reds saying earnestly to the reporter, 'In my opinion, and I'm sure the ACB would agree, sport is absolutely crucial for young indigenous Australians, whether they're playing at elite level or in the community. It's a healthy pastime, it's competitive, it's constructive and it gives them a real sense of pride.'

'And they can compete on equal terms?' suggested the reporter.

'In sport there's still not always a level playing field, but at least programmes like this are helping our people get on the field.'

'Thanks, that'll do. Best of luck today,' the reporter said, clicking off his tape recorder.

Lan hung back but managed to catch Jermaine's eye. The captain of the Dead Reds strolled over in response to his gesture. 'What's up, Lan-man? Didn't catch you at brekkie this morning. Too nervous to eat, hey?' He grinned.

'I've got to talk to you. In private.'

''Bout what?'

'The match, of course.'

Jermaine's face registered over-the-top amazement. He made a show of looking around him furtively. 'Hey, Lan-man, that's illegal. That's what they call match fixing. C'n get you into a whole heap of trouble. Ask Warnie.'

'It's not that! It's about one of our players. Where can we go?' Lan looked around and spotted a row of benches set up on the perimeter of the playing field. 'What about over there?'

An intrigued Jermaine followed him and they sat down on a bench facing the empty pitch. In a short while, Lan thought, he'd probably be out there sending down the first deliveries. The way his luck had gone all weekend, he couldn't bet on winning the toss. He scrutinised the pitch. The Dead Reds' coach had suggested it wasn't level, but it looked fine to him.

'OK, shoot,' Jermaine said. 'What's this kid's problem?'

Lan had rehearsed various openings during the bus ride to the grounds, but in none of them had he factored in such a direct first question — to which the obvious response was, 'This kid's problem is that he's a girl'. But that seemed to imply that just being a girl was a problem, and he was sure Sam didn't see it like that. In her eyes, the only problem was the organisers' failure to include girls in the carnival.

'I have to tell you some background first,' he began. 'This all happened because at the last minute one of our players, David, couldn't come to Melbourne.' He briefly recounted the story of how he had found another batsman, being careful not to give a name and to say 'he' or 'him'. 'It was only this morning that I found out something very very important about this player,' he said. He paused dramatically. He certainly had his listener's full attention.

'What?'

'She's a girl.'

'A *girl*? Are you kiddin' me, man? A real girl?'

What other kind was there, Lan wondered. 'Keep your voice down. Only me and Izzy, my vice captain, know.'

Jermaine tipped his head back and laughed uproariously. 'How'd you find out? Or shouldn't I ask?'

'Doesn't matter. The point is, what do we do now?'

'Who is it?' Jermaine asked.

Lan shook his head. 'It's not important. She doesn't play any differently from the rest of us Nips. We didn't spot it; neither did any of the other teams we've played. You wouldn't have either, I bet.'

'So what's your problem?'

'We can't simply replace her. Andy Chen, our fast bowler, is out sick so our twelfth man, Rikki Koh, is on today. If she can't play we'll be a man short.'

'And if she does play, you'll still be a man short,' Jermaine chortled. He seemed to find the whole situation very funny.

Lan acknowledged the joke with a weak smile. 'That's about it.'

'So let her play.'

'I would except — well, having a girl in the team could be against the rules. If we win today, I don't want the Nips to be disqualified because of that.'

'So here's what ya do if ya win today.' Jermaine's expression indicated he thought that unlikely. 'Don't tell anyone. Just take the Cup and shut up.'

'I couldn't do that. It wouldn't be an honest win.'

Jermaine looked a little perplexed. 'Well then, why doncha find out if it's against the rules? Go and ask that Laura girl from the ACB, she'll soon tell ya.'

'I can't risk it,' Lan explained. 'If she says it's not against the rules, that's fine. But what if she says it is? That means all the matches we've played so far might not count.'

'Nah.' Jermaine shook his head. 'They wouldn't do that. Anyway, you didn't know you had a girl on the team then, didya?'

'There's another reason,' Lan said. 'If it did turn out to be against the rules then S ... this person couldn't play in the match today. I don't mind being one short, but I'd like her to have the chance to show what she can do. Then her parents might let her play cricket.' Briefly, he explained Sam's situation.

'So why are you telling me all this now?' Jermaine asked when he'd finished.

'You're the opposing captain so I thought you

should know. If you say it's all right with you, nobody can say that's not fair, can they?'

'And what if I say I don't want to play against no girl?'

Lan shrugged. 'I might think you were chicken. I might think you were too scared to face her. She's pretty good.'

Jermaine's eyes narrowed. 'Listen, man, I'm Wangkunurra. Girls don't scare me.'

'Great! You won't have any problem with her playing then, right?'

Jermaine grunted and then said teasingly, 'You sure she's the *only* girl on your team, Lan-man? Maybe there's others you haven't uncovered yet.'

'Nup, I'm pretty sure she's the only one.' Lan stood up. 'I'd better go and tell her. Thanks, Jermaine. You'll keep all this to yourself, won't you?'

'You're not gunna tell me who she is?'

'Sorry.'

'I'll find out!'

'Good luck!'

Lan sped back to the Nips' changing room. Sam, dressed in the team uniform, was waiting outside the entrance. She looked at him anxiously. 'What did Jermaine say?'

'It's OK. You're in.'

A smile of relief transformed her face. 'Oh,

that's so great! Thanks, Lan. I won't let you down, you'll see. I had a feeling everything would work out. My Qi has felt very strong this morning.'

'Your what?'

'Qi. It's a Chinese word. It means a sort of flow of energy, like wind, or water. Very powerful.'

'Oh. Good.' He looked around and lowered his voice. 'Listen, Sam, he only knows one of our players is a girl, he doesn't know which one. I'm not going to tell the other Nips about you either, at least, not before the match. As far as they know, you're a boy, just like you've been the whole trip, OK?'

'Sure.'

'Jermaine'll probably try to pick who it is so don't stress out if you catch him staring. He doesn't know. Just be yourself.' He caught himself. 'I s'pose I really mean don't be yourself. Be who you've been all week.'

'I know what you mean. I'm getting used to it by now. But it's been a bit of a strain.'

'Yeah, I could see that. I knew something was bothering you.' Lan looked at his watch. 'Now I have to go in and motivate everyone and I've just about run out of motivational things to say. You use them up fast when you're playing every day. How does Steve Waugh do it?'

'Don't worry, Mr Thistleton's ahead of you. He's in there now, reading everyone a poem.'

'So that's why you're out here.'

She grinned. 'No! I just thought I should make myself scarce while people were getting changed.'

'Well, you've probably missed the poem. It's safe to go back in. C'mon.' He stopped suddenly, a look of anguish on his face. 'Oh no! I left my notes back at St Paul's! With all the fuss about Andy, I forgot to bring them.'

'You don't need notes,' Sam said. 'You know what to say by now.'

They went into the changing room and Lan discovered that she was right.

Nineteen

Much to Lan's surprise, he won the toss. 'We'll bat,' he said.

'Right,' said the umpire. 'Thirty-five overs, no bouncers, seven overs per bowler, batsmen retire at fifty.'

Jermaine nudged Lan as they walked off. 'Bats*men* retire at fifty,' he said, with emphasis. 'If your girl's real deadly, she could stay at the crease and get a century.'

'Sshhh.' Lan looked around nervously. 'You said you wouldn't say anything.'

'Just a joke, Lan-man. My lips are sealed.'

Lan looked again at Jermaine's lips. They were covered with a thick coating of white zinc cream. A stripe ran down the centre of his nose and there was a smear under each eye. 'You look like you're wearing warpaint,' he said.

Jermaine's eyes lit up. 'Hey, that's a wicked idea! Shoulda brought some red ochre with us. Think there's anything in the rules against paintin' yourself?'

Mention of the rules only increased the tension Lan was feeling. Was Jermaine deliberately playing mind games with him, trying to keep him on edge? He shrugged, and Jermaine laughed and thumped him on the back. He seemed in a very carefree mood.

'This is gunna be a deadly match, Lan-man,' he said. 'Let's have some fun.'

Lan couldn't remember an opponent saying that to him before. It was in stark contrast to the tense beginning of the Nips' match against King's XI, and the captain's cunning manipulation of the toss. But he suddenly remembered something Spinner had said to him on the train coming to Melbourne. He'd listened to Lan's ideas for daily team meetings, motivational sessions and putting in some extra practice each morning and night, and then the old man had scratched his chin and said,

'Matey, remember there's more to life than cricket. D'ya get what I'm sayin'?'

'That winning's not everything?'

Spinner nodded. 'Leave that serious win-at-all-costs stuff to the pros, they're gettin' paid for it. That's not to say you shouldn't want to win, mind, and you're doing a good job of keepin' everyone fired up, but don't let winnin' be the only consideration. Have fun while you're in Melbourne and enjoy the matches.'

Yes, Lan conceded; perhaps he'd temporarily forgotten about the fun and how much he loved playing. Understandable, of course, with the changes to the team and resulting tensions, not to mention the responsibility he felt as a touring captain. Now there was the added burden of Sam's secret and Andy's illness. Still, he resolved to do his best to put all of it out of his mind for the next few hours.

The end of the third over and none for seventeen: an excellent start, especially since Sam and Akram were up against Kingsley, the Reds' star bowler.

'He's a real speed merchant,' Lan said, watching from the team bench. 'Very quick through the crease, he almost slings it.' It was always handy for a fast bowler to be tall, he thought; if you had height, you could get bounce. Andy measured himself once a week and claimed he had grown three centimetres since their match against King's.

'He oughta be in a basketball team,' Izram said, relieved they'd agreed that Lan would bat third. The quickie might have delivered his quota by then or at least slackened off. 'How tall d'you reckon he is, anyway?'

'Bloody tall for thirteen,' Sal said.

'How d'ya know he's thirteen?'

'This is an under-fourteen competition so he can't be any older, can he?'

'Quickies are always good to watch, aren't they?' Lan observed. Despite his anxiety for Sam and Akram, he was enjoying these opening overs. The seagulls were back in their usual place around the wicket and he tried to spot the self-important fat one.

'The Reds look wicked,' Izram said. 'Wonder whose bright idea it was to decorate themselves with zinc cream?'

'Um, mine actually,' Lan confessed.

'*Yours?*'

They looked at him in surprise, and Lan explained.

'Well, well!' Sal said slyly. 'If it gives them a psychological advantage we'll know who to blame, won't we, Captain?'

Eight overs gone, none for forty-five. At the crease, Sam waited. Jermaine began his spell of bowling. Sam played a sweep shot and it was well-fielded at square leg. No run.

Next ball; a forward defensive shot and still looking for a run.

A delivery outside the off stump, and an easy single which brought Akram on strike.

Next delivery, and Akram went to swing it down the leg side but got a bottom edge. The keeper took the catch, to the explosive jubilation of the Dead Reds and their supporters and the groans of the Nips.

'Jeez, what's that noise?' Sal asked, looking up at the trees. 'Kookaburras?'

'A didjeridoo,' Lan answered, getting to his feet. 'Magic, huh? It's over there.' He pointed with his bat to a large and exuberant group sprawled on the grass underneath the gum trees on the eastern boundary.

'Wow, that some stick!' Tomas exclaimed.

Akram out for twenty, Sam sitting on thirty-three. Lan walked to the crease.

'Ya like the didj?' Jermaine called to him.

'Deadly!' Lan replied, fastening his helmet.

'He's gettin' ready to play it again, Lan-man.'

'Tell him not to hold his breath.'

Jermaine grinned. From the non-striker's end, Sam gave him a thumbs-up.

Lan took guard. He asked the umpire for centre, and looked around the field, noting the placements and the gaps. There … there … and there. That's where he'd score runs.

Take it easy, he told himself. Play yourself in.

Jermaine bowled the last two balls of the over, the final one a stock leggie. Lan forgot about playing himself in and smashed it through cover for a boundary. There was a huge cheer and applause from the spectators.

And something else.

For a moment, Lan thought it was the St Paul's meal gong that somebody had brought to the ground to announce the lunch break. But it was too early for lunch. Then a drum and bells joined in, and Sam was grinning and pointing to a lively crowd in front of the pavilion and a banner that read 'Australian-Chinese Association, Eastern Suburbs'. Along with their chairs and picnic rugs, they had brought an assortment of musical instruments. Another group on the perimeter waved a Vietnamese flag and yelled encouragement.

Lan was astounded. He hoped Izram was taking photographs. This was definitely something he wanted his parents to see!

He and Sam formed a good partnership, playing well together and putting runs on the board. Sam was on forty-three and Lan on strike at twenty-eight when Jermaine recalled his fast bowler, Kingsley for his final over. The message was clear: do something about these two.

Kingsley came racing down the pitch, the scowl on his face made more ferocious by the stripes of zinc cream. Lan experienced a brief flash of panic but managed to chop it away for a single.

Sam on strike now. Again, Kingsley raced in. It was a sharp rising delivery and Sam swivelled, twisting her head, and tried to hook. But she wasn't quite in a position to play it. The ball slammed into her helmet.

From the other end, Lan heard the crack as it hit the grille. At least, he hoped it was the grille.

The umpire was signalling 'No ball' as Sam fell to the ground.

The spectators gasped. The Nips on the bench jumped to their feet. Lan dropped his bat and ran to the wicket.

Sam was struggling to her feet before he got there. How was she managing to stand? Lan wondered.

'Are you OK?'

'Yeah. The grille took most of the impact,' Sam gasped.

'Like hell it did.' He helped her remove the helmet. A massive bruise was erupting around her left ear, just below the temple. A few extra centimetres and it would have got her eye.

Kingsley came up. 'Jeez, sorry, man. You OK?'

'That was a bouncer,' Lan said accusingly.

Sam shook her head, wincing with the pain as she did so. 'My fault. Shouldn't have tried to play it.'

A runner came up and thrust a bottle of water into her hand. She took a long swig and then moved her jaw experimentally. 'See, not broken,' she said, trying to smile.

A first-aid attendant came onto the pitch and examined the bruise. 'Lucky,' he said. 'With an ice pack on that, you'll probably get away with nothing more than just a massive headache. But I'd like to check you over.' He advised her to come off.

'No,' Sam said.

The umpire said it might be the wisest thing to do. Lan agreed.

'I want a word with my captain,' Sam muttered. She pulled Lan aside and spoke in a harsh whisper. 'First off, I want to get my fifty. Second, I don't want anyone examining me, thanks very much.'

'Sam, it's a head injury,' Lan whispered back. 'Where d'you think they're gonna examine you?'

'Who knows? They might tell me to take my shirt off. They might want to listen to my heart or check my reflexes or something. I can't risk it.'

'You shouldn't risk your brain, either. You might have concussion.'

'It's just a little bang on the side of my head. Don't worry.'

Lan couldn't help worrying. The bruise looked nasty. But he knew that in similar circumstances he too would want to play on.

From the Nips' bench the other members of the team were watching anxiously.

'He's putting on his helmet … he's going to play on,' Akram said.

'He wants to get his fifty,' Sal said.

'Sam a tough bugger,' Tomas said.

Yes, Izram thought admiringly. She certainly was.

Play continued but Sam was run out shortly after and dismissed for forty-five. Lan could see by her face how painful running was; every footfall must deliver a jar to the head. He could see, too, how much she minded missing that half-century.

'A great innings, Sam,' he assured her. 'You oughta be proud.'

She walked off to a huge ovation, the gongs and cymbals booming and crashing and the spectators on their feet, applauding.

Izram came out to join Lan. 'Some burn,' he said nervously.

'Yeah,' said Lan, even more nervously. He was on strike and Kingsley still had two deliveries left in the over. One batsman down, one to go, that's what he'd be thinking. At the other end of the pitch, Kingsley gave the ball a vigorous polish and began his run in. Lan licked his lips. No doubt about it: fast bowlers were *scary*.

But before the thought could overpower him, he told himself to get a grip. What was there to be scared of? When his mother was seventeen, she had escaped with her younger sister and brother from the bloody streets of Saigon and sailed to Indonesia in a rusty and leaking boat. His father had fought the Communists and walked alone through jungles and across rivers to a refugee camp. And *he*, their son, was scared of a *boy bowling a ball*?

Lan squared his shoulders and waited for whatever delivery came his way.

At the end of overs, the Nips had posted a score of eight for 188. Lan was the only player to retire with fifty; Izram had got twenty-six before his lbw and Satria, on sixteen, had scored his highest number of runs ever. Hiroki's despair over his duck was balanced by Rikki's amazement at still being alive, and what was even more amazing, not out. He'd sat on the bench for almost two hours, terrified at the prospect of going in. When his time finally came, he'd been in a near panic when he couldn't find his gloves. 'You're sitting on them,' Izram had pointed out.

He hadn't even seen the first ball and had looked around to see what had happened to it. 'Is this what you're looking for?' the wicket-keeper had said with a grin. The next ball had thudded into his stomach; the third had whizzed past on the edge of his vision and the fourth almost knocked him off his feet. The fifth hit his glove and trickled away for a single. Rikki had got to the other end and sighed with relief.

Lan was moderately pleased with their score but knew they had a tough task ahead of them. Andy was still back in bed at St Paul's and Sam was really in no shape to take on seven overs of bowling. He called an impromptu team meeting before they went to lunch and outlined his strategy.

'I'll bowl seven, of course, and so will Roki and Onya.'

'And I'll bowl seven!' Sam said firmly, clutching an ice pack to her temple.

Lan shook his head. 'Not a good idea, Sam.'

'I'm fine. The St John's guy said I was fine.'

'He didn't say you were *fine*,' Lan corrected. 'He said you had a nasty bump and you should take it easy.'

'I'll bowl an over at a time.'

'I don't think you should bowl at all. Even fielding's dodgy, but I'll put you near the boundary and hopefully you won't get many balls.'

'The boundary?' Sam's face fell.

'That leaves fifteen overs. Akka and Phon, reckon you can handle some?'

'Sure.' Their faces radiated confidence.

'Sal, Satto, Jemmo, might be calling on you, too.'

They nodded, although at least one of them was thinking that if things ever got that desperate the Nips were in a bad way.

'And me,' Rikki said bravely. He wore an expression that must have been seen on the faces of countless shell-shocked soldiers before they leapt out of the trenches to attack the machine guns on the Western front.

'Thanks, Rikki, we'll see how it goes,' Lan said. 'Thanks, everyone. We'll have to pull together to win this one.'

'Give me at least a few overs,' Sam pleaded, as the others headed towards the pavilion. 'I've had a good rest on the bench and see, the ice pack's working already.' She lowered her voice. 'You're treating me differently because I'm a girl.'

'I'm not!' Lan protested, and then immediately wondered if he was.

Sam touched his arm. '*Please*, Lan?'

Lan felt himself weakening. Girls knew how to get to you. He always found Linh much harder to resist than Tien.

'Maybe one or two,' he said. 'I'll see how it goes.'

Sam beamed. 'Thanks, Lan.'

'Lie down in the change room during the break and keep that icepack on. I'll get some sandwiches for you.'

Sam promised to rest and they left her and caught up with the others in the pavilion. 'There's Spinner,' Izram said. 'Who's that with him?'

The coach had arrived at the ground in time to see Lan get his half-century, and had told them that while Andy was on the road to recovery, he wasn't quite there yet. What Spinner'd been doing since then had been something of a mystery. Usually he sat with them and analysed the play. Today, just when Lan felt most in need of his advice, they'd hardly seen him. Was this the reason?

He saw them and waved them over. 'Mateys,' he said, 'Meet Shirley.'

Shirley? Lan looked at the small woman with soft silver-grey hair smiling by his side. Was this Grace's rival? So that was why he had dressed so smartly this morning. The other Nips were equally surprised. When had Spinner ever brought a lady to a cricket match?

'Clarrie,' the lady admonished gently, 'that's not much of an introduction.'

'Sorry, I'm forgettin' me manners,' he said. 'Lads, I'd like you to meet Mrs Shirley Pringle.'

'Call me Shirl,' she said.

Spinner introduced them by name, and when he got to Lan, she said, 'Oh, you're the captain. The one who phoned to tell Clarrie nobody had drowned.' Lan nodded, fascinated by her dimples. 'Clarrie's told me so much about you all,' she went on. 'I feel I know you already.'

Lan and Izram exchanged glances. Clarrie certainly hadn't been as chatty about her! Lan seized the chance to find out more. 'Have you known Spinner long … um, Shirl?' he asked.

'We met nearly fifty years ago, dear,' she said, shattering Lan's hopes that Grace might have got in first and thus have a prior claim. 'Clarrie and my husband used to play cricket together.'

'You've got a husband?' Izram asked hopefully.

'Not now, dear. It's wonderful to meet Clarrie again. You know, it's been forty years or more since I last saw him.'

'Why did you wait such a long time?' Lan asked. 'Melbourne's not that far from Adelaide.'

Mrs Pringle laughed and looked as if she was quite ready to tell them but Spinner had had enough of the questions. 'The break's nearly over, lads,' he interrupted. 'Better get yerselves some tucker.'

'You'd better have something to eat, too, Clarrie,' Mrs Pringle said. 'You've had a busy morning. Sit down and I'll get you some salad.'

Lan and Izram exchanged another glance. Since when did Spinner eat salad? 'She's a bit bossy,' Izram whispered, as they headed towards the buffet table.

'She's not as pretty as Grace,' Lan said. 'She's nice, though.'

'She's a lot older,' Izram said.

'But Spinner's old, too, so that's all right.'

Izram frowned at him. 'It's not all right if Grace's back in Adelaide being faithful and he's here running around with another lady.'

'Well, he might not be thinking of marrying her,' Lan said. He selected some sandwiches and put them on a plate for Sam.

'He'd better not,' Izram said darkly. 'We don't want him moving to Melbourne. I think we oughta tell Grace about this Mrs Pringle when we get home.'

'Mmm,' said Lan, rather losing interest in the conversation. He had weightier things on his mind than Spinner's love life.

Twenty

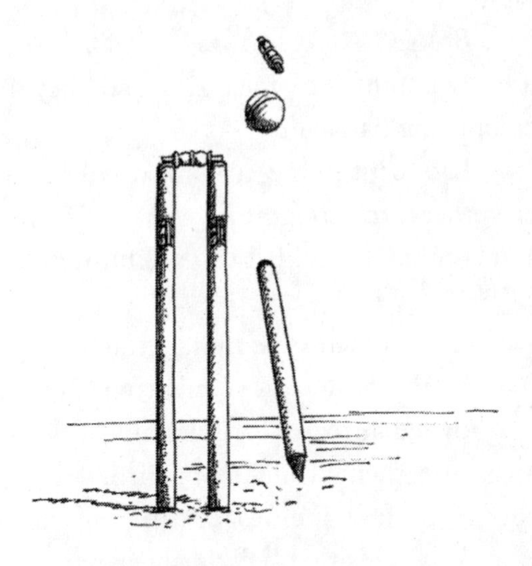

The opposition managed to score only two runs off Lan's first over, which gave his confidence a huge boost — Andy normally opened the bowling — and the Nips a great start. The first ball of his second over was short on the off side. The Reds' batsman cut it to the boundary for four, and the didjeridoo kookaburras blasted out across the ground. Lan found the sound rather less magical this time. He took a deep breath and tried to focus. Giving away fours was not in his game plan.

His next ball pitched in the same place. Lan grimaced, anticipating another four as the batsman moved in to repeat the shot. But Sal had already moved to the right in anticipation and took a terrific catch.

Bowled Nguyen caught Catano ... less than fifteen minutes into the game and they'd removed the opening batsman!

Lan leapt in the air with delight and ran with the others to congratulate Sal. 'We're building momentum,' he told them gleefully. 'Let's keep it up.'

Alas, some of the momentum began to trickle away as the Reds recovered from their early loss. Lan bowled three overs, claiming a wicket in his third, and then brought on Hiroki who, eager to redeem his first innings duck, enthusiastically ran up to deliver his first ball, mismeasured, and arrived at the crease with his right foot forward. If he had been a left-handed bowler, all would have been well, but he was right-handed. He tried to pull himself up, failed, and the ball left his hand and soared skywards. Laughter echoed around the ground, which in itself was enough to shatter Hiroki's fragile confidence, let alone the fact that the grinning batsman, with a fine horizontal sweep at the critical moment, sent the ball flying towards the boundary.

Lan felt for him and ran in to give him some words of encouragement. Now suffering a bad attack of nerves, Hiroki served up a series of long-hops and full tosses to the grateful batsmen. As the runs began to pile up alarmingly, Lan took him off and brought on Tomas. With his third ball of his first over, Tomas took the wicket, a feat that seemed to surprise him as much as it did the second batsman.

'Onya, Onya!' yelled the fielders, rushing up to slap him on the back.

It was the last breakthrough for a long time.

'Bring me on,' Sam pleaded at the drinks break.

Lan was momentarily tempted. Three for 119 and fifteen overs to go. He had three left, and he ought to keep at least one of those for when things got really desperate. At the moment, they were only approaching desperate. An extra wicket or two would be very handy right now. But he wouldn't risk Sam's injuries, even if she herself was willing to. Partially shaded by her hat, the bruise was looking more and more like a fried egg burnt around the edges, and he'd noted the painkillers she'd swallowed with her drink. She really ought to be lying down in a dark room, resting.

'You're doing great on the boundary, Sam,' he assured her. 'You've saved lots of runs.'

'Let me bowl and we can save the match,' she urged.

He shook his head. They didn't need a win that bad. He sent in Sal.

Lan kept shuffling through his bowlers and the batsmen survived. The runs mounted, the Reds playing a fast aggressive game with some good individual performances in the middle order. Lan felt proud of his team: the fielders were alert and the bowlers were doing their best, but their lack of experience told. With three overs remaining and only one more wicket taken — Satria had claimed an lbw in the twenty-first over — it was clearly now or never. The score stood at 4/167; the Reds needed only twenty-two more for victory. Jermaine was at the non-striker's end, full of good-humoured confidence and sitting on thirty-two.

'Back again, Lan-man? Hope you got some trick balls up your sleeve, you gunna need 'em.'

'Saving the trickiest for you, Jerms,' Lan answered easily.

'Ya don't scare me, Lan-man.'

'Then why are ya looking so pale?'

'Good one!' Jermaine laughed delightedly. 'Hey, I reckon I've spotted your ring-in.'

'Bet you haven't.' Lan stepped out for his run-up, polishing the ball and trying to detach his mind from everything but the task ahead.

He launched into his run and sent the ball down hard and fast. It took the edge of the bat and soared towards third man … towards Hiroki.

Oh no, thought Lan. Not Roki!

Hiroki ran and dived on the ball. Grass and bits of turf flew everywhere. 'He's caught it!' Izram yelled.

The Nips ran towards him. 'Goodonya!' … 'Great catch, Roki!'

Hiroki seemed stunned. He got to his feet. 'Who did I catch? Who's out?'

Lan thumped him on the back and grinned. Sometimes, Hiroki didn't seem to be on the same planet.

Five for 177. Lan sent down his next delivery with grim determination. The batsman hit it for four valuable runs that put the Reds in sight of victory, something that spurred their supporters to even wilder expressions of encouragement.

Lan gritted his teeth. He'd heard the expression before but had never quite known what it meant. Now he did. He sent down a fast, rising ball that clipped the edge of the bat and flew like a bullet, low and about three metres from Sal's right. Sal flung himself at it and, airborne, caught it just above the ground. Bewdie!

Six for 181. The new batsman came in and hit a single, and Jermaine now faced Lan.

Lan took a deep breath and sent down his next delivery. Jermaine played it, the ball racing towards the boundary. Jermaine streaked down the pitch and Sam, impossibly far away, ran like mad. She dived forward and rolled, the ball in her hand. The fielders whooped and cheered. A magnificent catch in any circumstances. Given Sam's condition, a bloody miracle!

Elated, Lan made an energetic appeal as applause rang out across the ground and the Chinese gong boomed. Jermaine, obviously disappointed, began to walk off.

With only five balls remaining, the Nips now stood a chance. Lan was sure they could contain the runs now Jermaine was gone.

Sam had scrambled to her feet. It took her a moment to realise what the situation was but when she did she hurled the ball back to Lan. 'Not out!' she called.

'You sure?'

'It touched the ground,' Sam yelled.

Despite his disappointment, Lan didn't hesitate. 'Hey, Captain,' he called to Jermaine's retreating back. 'Where d'ya think you're going? Come back and finish your innings!' He turned to the umpire. 'That's right, isn't it?'

The umpire nodded. 'Good show. Not out! Play on.'

A ripple of applause spread across the ground as the spectators told each other what had happened.

Reprieved from sudden death, Jermaine jogged back to the wicket and decided caution might be in order. He took a safe single, only belatedly realising this would bring his batting partner on strike.

Six to win, four balls to go.

Lan nodded to Izram. His wicket-keeper nodded back.

Lan flighted the ball down towards the leg stump. It hit the pitch and spun towards middle stump. The batsman attempted to play the ball but sent a catch into the outstretched hands of Izram as he leapt sideward.

Lan jumped in the air with excitement. *Howzat!* The finger went up and he and a jubilant Izram hugged each other as the other fielders ran to join them.

'Jeez, the tension's killing me,' Izram said.

'*You're* tense?'

On came the Reds' next batsman, the weight of responsibility heavy on his shoulders.

Six to win, three balls to go.

The incoming batsman had evidently decided that no matter what happened, he was going to run. Unfortunately, this strategy hadn't been communicated to his captain at the other end. He tapped the ball away and took off, forgetting to yell, 'Yes'. He was more than halfway down the pitch when, taken by surprise, Jermaine started his run.

At cover, Phon had intercepted the ball and hurled it back towards the wicket. Izram took the ball in his gloves and went for the bails. Jermaine stretched out his bat but his luck had run out. He missed the line by centimetres.

It was a huge dismissal. We can do it, Lan thought. We *can!*

With the knowledge that the bowler was on a hat-trick and the end was in sight, the musicians in the crowd decided to stage their own battle. The resulting cacophony was obviously too much for one small terrier who suddenly shot onto the field, scattering the seagulls, and evading all attempts by his owner to reclaim him.

It eased the tension. Lan grinned, suddenly reminded of Larri. Both batsmen smiled and Izram yelled advice as nearby fielders dived for the dog.

When order was restored, Lan prepared to

bowl his next to last ball. He licked his lips. This was the time to deliver. Could he do it?

It pitched up, the batsman took a huge swing, connected and hit it high. A six?

Sam! Sam! Lan prayed silently.

On the boundary, Sam was moving into position, her eyes never leaving the ball, her hands up ... and a beautiful catch!

The noise from the spectators was deafening, but Lan hardly heard it. His first hat-trick! His excitement peaked as his jubilant team-mates encircled him.

'We're gonna win this!' Izram cried, thumping him on the back.

Lan nodded, but suspected he was too fired up. He told himself to calm down and refocus on the game. He took deep breaths as he walked back for his run-up.

At the crease, the new batsman scowled with fierce determination. With one ball to go and five to win, there was nothing to be gained by mere survival: he would finish in a blaze of glory.

Lan suddenly remembered one of Spinner's stories about a similar situation some twenty years ago. With one ball to go and New Zealand poised to win the match, the Australian captain had instructed Greg Chappell to bowl the last ball underarm. It had been within the rules and it had won Australia the match, but Spinner said that it hadn't been cricket.

Lan said a little prayer and sent down a standard leggie. The batsman slashed wildly, but it was not to be his day. It went through slips for two, and the match was over.

Amid the applause and celebrations, Jermaine was the first to sprint onto the field. 'That was magic! Best game we ever had, brother! And what about your hat-trick, Lan-man?' He put his arm around Lan's shoulder. 'You Nips are deadly. You come to Alice anytime and give us another game, OK?'

Lan had picked up the ball and now gave it to Sam as a souvenir. 'You were awesome,' he said. 'I wouldn't be surprised if you won Man-of-the-Match.'

Sam laughed. 'I would be!'

Spinner, bursting with pride, went onto the field to congratulate them. He shook hands with both captains. 'You blokes had me on the edge of me seat,' he said. 'Blimey, I haven't seen a match as exciting as that since '93 when Australia lost by one run to the West Indies at Adelaide Oval.'

'Was that 1893, Spinner?' Izram asked cheekily, and everybody grinned.

'One run not very big difference,' Tomas said.

'Enough to lose by,' Jermaine said, a little despondently.

'It was a good game,' Spinner told him. 'Y'can all be proud of yerselves.'

'I am. We are,' Jermaine said.

'It was a terrific match,' Lan agreed, as they walked off the field. He couldn't resist a little skip. So this was what victory felt like! The release of tension was wonderful.

'Everyone did their bit,' Sam said.

'How's your poor old head?'

'Almost recovered.' She grinned at him. 'Good thing you kept me on the boundary, wasn't it?'

At the pavilion, they were surrounded by well-wishers. Everyone was beaming and exclaiming what a great match it had been, how close, what a nail-biting end. Russell and some of the Hunters crowded around. 'You were awesome, we were all barracking for you,' Russell told Lan.

'Really? I thought you'd be cheering for the Reds.' Why did he think that? Only because the Tiwi team was black.

'Nah. They were a bit up themselves and you Nips put on a really good fight.'

Lan grinned. As he'd once told his mother, Australians liked to barrack for the battlers.

A Vietnamese woman with two children came up and gave him a shy smile. 'Lan Nguyen?' she said.

He looked at her, surprised. She was a complete stranger. 'Yes?' he said.

'You play so wonderful. My children would like autograph, please?'

'*Mine?*'

'We enjoy game very much. We hope one day you famous, play cricket for Australia.'

Lan blushed. He took the pen she handed him and the children, a boy of about eight and a younger girl, looked at him in awe as he signed their programmes.

'This is Hung and this is Tu Anh.'

'Do you play cricket, Hung?' Lan asked

'Not yet,' the boy said. 'But now I want to learn.'

'Me too,' said Tu Anh.

'I've got a sister like you,' Lan said.

They thanked him and as they turned to leave, the woman took his hand and said something in Vietnamese.

'You're blushing again,' Izram said. 'What did she say?'

'Nothing much. Hey, I gave my first autographs!'

Izram gave him a shove. 'Oh, you are sooo famous, big head!'

Lan grinned and shoved him back. Suddenly, he felt very very happy.

'Hey, look who's here!' Akram exclaimed.

It was Mr Thistleton, and by his side, Andy.

Everybody was delighted to see him on his feet and looking, if not in radiant health, at least a lot brighter than he'd been that morning.

'Splendid work, boys!' Mr Thistleton said. 'We caught most of the second half. You all played jolly well, especially you, Lan. What about that hat-trick! Something to be proud of, eh?'

'It was a tough match,' Andy said. 'I feel really bad I let you down.'

'Wasn't your fault,' Lan said. 'And we wouldn't have made the finals anyway if it hadn't been for you.'

Andy cheered up.

Laura Jolly came over. 'Congratulations, Nips! What an exciting game! We couldn't have asked for a better one. Don't go away, will you? We're having the prize-giving soon.'

Izram tugged Lan's arm. 'Are you gonna tell her about Sam?' he whispered.

With a start, Lan realised he'd forgotten all about that little problem. He had to tell her, of course, even if it meant disqualification. His spirits sank. How easy it had been *before* the match to decide on the noble course of action and how difficult, now that the Cup was within his grasp. What would Laura say? What would his team-mates say?

'Laura, there's something I have to tell you,' he said.

Sam looked at him in alarm and shook her head.

'Can it wait?' Laura said. 'The presentation's about to start.' She gestured towards the front of the pavilion where a table and microphones had been set up. 'Look, there's the Harmony Cup. Aren't you excited? Got your speech ready?'

'It's about one of our players,' Lan said, taking Sam's arm and giving her a reassuring nod.

Laura seemed not to hear. 'And you'll never guess who's here to present the prizes?' She beamed at him. 'Ricky Ponting!'

Twenty-one

Captain's Diary: Sunday 21 January (late)
The Overland, Melbourne-Adelaide

It has been a long day full of excitement and surprises and I am glad it is nearly over because I don't think I can take any more day or any more excitement or any more surprises. After I get home I'll write up the details of our final match but my brain is too tired to do it now.

One of the surprises was this: it turned out that all through the carnival, people from the ACB had been on the lookout for promising players, who all got invitations to attend special coaching clinics when they got home. I got one, and so did Jermaine and Kingsley, and I was glad for them both because they are good players and I reckon Kingsley might even turn out to be another Eddie Gilbert! Andy, Izram and Sal all got invitations — and so did Sam. I was doubly glad then that I had told Laura Jolly the truth about Sam. (Note: add bits about how found out about Sam. Too tired now.)

Sam wasn't keen to confess. I guess she was nervous that the Cup would be taken away from us and everybody would blame her. But when we told Laura, what a surprise! She said it wasn't actually against the rules. She said in some places where there weren't enough girls to make up a team, they often played in boys' teams.

Sam said, 'Great! So I can still play with the Nips,' and Laura said, 'Sam, why don't you think about playing women's cricket? I can put you in touch with people in Adelaide who'll help you.' Sam thanked her, but I could see that she really wanted to go on playing with the Nips, so I said she could. After her great performance, I didn't think any of the team would object, and I thought she'd be a real inspiration for little girls like Linh and Tu Anh.

Jermaine was disappointed that the Dead Reds didn't win the Cup, of course, but I reminded him of the Aussies' long struggle to win the World Cup and how they never gave up and because of that they are now world champions. In my speech I said that our team song was true — the Nips are getting bigger — and next year we would be ENORMOUS, and everybody applauded.

I think I'm getting better at making speeches but it is still scary. Even more scary — there was Ricky Ponting holding the Harmony Cup and waiting for me to come and collect it! My heart was pounding, and not just because I had to make a speech. I thought, will he recognise me? Will he say, 'Wait a minute, aren't you the kid I caught vandalising the MCG pitch last Friday?'

I walked to the microphone trying to look very happy. Not just because we were getting the winners' trophy but because Ricky Ponting hadn't seen me happy and smiling before and my mother says it changes my face a lot. He handed me the Cup and shook my hand and said that the Nips had put up a heroic fight and that was good for the spectators and good for cricket and we were sure to be an inspiration for ethnic kids all round the country, and I just kept smiling like an idiot. At one point he gave me a funny little look as if he might be thinking, 'Where have I seen you before?' but I made my speech and escaped.

I was breathing a sigh of relief when the Man of the Match award was announced. And it was me! I had to go back again! Ricky Ponting shook my hand again and gave me this big silver cup and said a lot of terrific things about my cricket, but he was looking at me and then he said, 'Didn't I meet you at the MCG on Friday?' My heart sank and I thought, here it comes, he's going to take back the cup and say, 'No way! We're not giving a prize to someone who digs up the hallowed turf,' and I would be shamed and my family dishonoured. My mouth went dry but I managed to say yes, he had, and that he had autographed my bat and that had given me good luck. And he SMILED and said he was GLAD and he hoped one day he would see me at the MCG again, PLAYING FOR AUSTRALIA.

As soon as we get home I am going to put a poster of Ricky Ponting up on my bedroom wall.

There was one more surprise. Jermaine came up after the awards and said, 'I know who the girl is.' And I said, 'Who do you think it is then?' and he said, 'That one.' And it wasn't Sam! Then he confessed that there was someone on his team who was breaking the rules too, because he was probably over fourteen. I said, 'I bet I know who it is. Kingsley, right?' and Jermaine said it wasn't Kingsley. I said, 'What do you mean probably? Doesn't this person know how old he is?' and Jermaine said nobody was sure because some Aborigines didn't have birth certificates. I said that was all right then and it had been a fair match. Jermaine said, 'Look out next year!' Then we exchanged shirts and I signed his and he signed mine.

We gave Spinner his new tie before the barbecue that ended the carnival. He looked at it and didn't say anything for so long I finally said, 'Do you like it, Spinner?' and he said 'Is the Pope Catholic?' He put it on right away and said it was real flash, the smartest thing in his wardrobe. Mrs Pringle said it made him look very handsome, so Sam was right: clothes do improve your sex appeal.

Once we were on the train home, I got up and told everyone the truth about Sam. Talk about a bombshell! Some people wouldn't believe it. I thought they were going to insist she got her gear off right then and there and prove it! Mr Thistleton was well surprised. 'Just like Agnodice,' he kept saying. We all said, 'Who?' and he said 'Didn't anyone listen to anything I said in Ancient History?' And then I remembered about the Greek woman who had disguised herself as a man in order to be a doctor.

But Spinner nodded and said, 'I thought there was a fair chance. When I was checkin' that bruise of yours, Sam, I noticed yer ears were pierced. Both of 'em. How many blokes have two pierced ears?' I was totally wrong about him. There is not much he misses.

About eleven o'clock Mr Thistleton got up and said that he and Spinner were going off to get nightcaps and he trusted us to behave ourselves while they were away. I thought this was a funny thing to get. So did Onya. After they'd gone he said, 'What is nightcap?' I said, 'It's probably something they give out on trains to help you sleep, like eye masks and earplugs on planes.'

'It's to keep your head warm if you're bald,' said Satto. This made sense because Mr Thistleton hasn't got much hair. But when they came back they didn't have anything on their heads. Perhaps they'd run out of night-caps.

Monday 22 January (early)
Adelaide

Our families were at the station to meet us and so excited to see the Cup! (We were waving it out the window as the train pulled into the station.) Grace was there too — with Larri. She must have missed Spinner a lot, perhaps even more than Larri did. Izram and I didn't know what to say to her. Izram said to me, 'It's a bit much, one lady at the station in Melbourne to see him off and another in Adelaide to welcome him home.'

We decided to break the news to her gently. So while Spinner was checking the bags I said, 'Grace, Spinner's got a girlfriend in Melbourne,' and she didn't look surprised at all. She said, 'Yes, I know, isn't it romantic?' And then she told us that Spinner had been in love with Shirley a long time ago but she had married another cricketer and he had married someone else and they had lost touch. But then Shirley read about him and how he was coaching us and she wrote a letter to him care of the Illaba Library (the letter we saw in Spinner's kitchen!), and said she would really love to meet him again and hoped he would come to Melbourne.

Grace said, 'He was very nervous about seeing her again. He thought it was too late.' I said, 'Too late for what?' and she said, 'Well, everything, I suppose,' but Izram nudged me and whispered 'Getting married'. I said to Grace, 'Do you think it's too late?' and she said, 'I don't think it's *ever* too late,' so maybe they will, who knows? It is not Mrs Pringle's fault that she lives in Melbourne. We all want Spinner to be happy.

I said, 'We thought you and Spinner were in love, Grace,' and she sort of spluttered and looked totally astonished. I said, 'What did you think when he sent you the flowers then?' She said, 'He didn't send me any flowers.' I said, 'Well, the radio station sent them but I told them to sign the card Mystery Spinner so you'd think they came from him.'

She looked puzzled but then she laughed and laughed so much that people on the platform turned to look at her. And guess what that dopey radio producer had done? Signed the card Miss T. Spinner. Grace thought the flowers were from a borrower pleased with the service at Illaba Library!

My mother is right. If you want something done properly, you have to do it yourself. She was there on the platform, waiting for me. The whole family was there. I showed them my Man of the Match cup and my parents were very proud, even though I know they want me to be a businessman or a doctor, not a cricketer.

But things have a way of working out for the best in the end, so I am hopeful.

About everything.

Glossary

Appeal. An umpire won't give a batsman out until a fielder or the bowler appeals, usually by yelling 'Howzat!' An appeal covers all ways of getting out and can be made until the time the bowler begins his run up for his next delivery. The fielding captain may ask for a withdrawal of an appeal, and the umpire may cancel his decision if he considers it justified. Excessive appealing is frowned on.

Ashes. The trophy awarded to the winner of a Test series between Australia and England (but permanently kept at Lord's Cricket Ground in London).

Baggy green. Baggy green cap worn by Australian Test cricketers.

Bails. Pair of turned pieces of wood, balanced on grooves at the top of the three stumps. A delivery that is knocked on to the wicket from bat or person, and removes the bails, has bowled the batsman.

Bodyline. A steep-rising delivery aimed at the batsman's body, first employed by English bowlers during the 1932-33 Ashes tour in an attempt to limit Don Bradman's runs.

Bouncer. A delivery from a fast bowler which hits the pitch half-way down and then bounces very high, at or near the head of the batsman.

Box. A protective device made of heavy-duty plastic, designed to protect the genitals of male cricketers.

Burn. Cricketers' jargon for a nasty bruise on the head from a bouncer.

Caught behind. A catch taken by the wicket-keeper.

Cover/s. A position where you put your most athletic fielder to run, dive, sprint and leap to catch those balls that would otherwise go straight to the boundary in a 'cover drive'.

Crease, bowling. The line drawn through the stumps.

Crease, popping. The line drawn on the pitch in front of the stumps.

Cricket, not. Unsporting behaviour.

Delivery. Any ball bowled to the batsman.

Duck. No score, an innings of no runs. Also called a blob, a quack, a zero.

Edge. To hit the ball on the sides of the bat, rather than the middle of the blade.

Fast bowlers. Also known as speed merchants and quicks, these are the bowlers who start their run-ups way, way back, race in at a fast trot, and fling the ball at speeds almost impossible to see. Brett Lee is currently Australia's (if not the world's) fastest bowler.

Flight. The direction of the ball through the air. Spin bowlers try to deceive the batsman by flighting the ball so that it drifts away in the air or drops suddenly.

Flipper. A ball from a leg spin bowler which, instead of spinning into or away from the batsman, goes straight. Shane Warne is master of the flipper.

Full toss. Balls that don't hit the pitch before they reach the batsman, and are relatively easy to hit for runs.

Googly. Also called a wrong 'un: deliveries which look like ordinary leg breaks to the batsman, but which spin the other way.

Guard. A mark on the ground, made by the batsman, so he knows where he's standing in regard to the stumps. Guard is given by the umpire.

Hat trick. Three dismissals in three consecutive balls.

Hook shot. An attacking shot played to a fast ball which arrives about head height.

Lbw. Leg before wicket; a method of dismissing a batsman where the ball hits the pads or leg in direct line with the stumps and is thus prevented from hitting the stumps. The ball can't have touched the bat first.

Leg-break, leggie. Ball that spins from the leg side (the side of the cricket field to the left of the batsman as he faces the bowler).

Line. The direction of a delivery; the path of the ball from the bowler's hand to where it hits the pitch. A good line means bowling at the stumps to hit them.

Long hop. A ball which lands halfway down the pitch and bounces at a comfortable height, giving the batsman plenty of time to get into position to hit it wherever he wants.

On (leg) side/offside. Depends whether the batsman is right or left-handed. When he takes up his stance facing the bowler, the side his legs are on is the leg side; the side his bat is on is the offside.

On strike. The batsman facing the bowler.

Over. Six deliveries from one end by a bowler.

Run up. The bowler's approach.

Silly. A field placing very close to the bat; (you'd have to be silly to stand there).

Sledging. Attempting to put off or intimidate an opposition player by making unfavourable comments.

Slips. Fielding position close to the bat on the offside, placed to catch any edged shot (usually the result of a mistake, snick or 'slip') from the batsman. First slip is next to the wicket-keeper; second, third and fourth further around.

Slogger. A bash artist; a batsman who tries to hit the ball as far as possible.

Snick. The sound the ball makes when it catches the edge of the bat.

Twelfth Man. The 'reserve'; (a cricket team has eleven players).

Walk, to. What a batsman does (or should do) when he knows he's out, and without waiting for the umpire's decision.

Wicket (1). The actual set of stumps and bails.

Wicket (2). The innings of a pair of batsmen. The first wicket is when the first of the opening batsmen is out.

Wisden. Wisden's Cricketer's Almanack comes out annually and records everything that has happened in cricket that year. A fast bowler called John Wisden started it in the nineteenth century.

Yorker. A ball that pitches near the batsman's feet and has to be 'dug out'; very difficult to score from.